FOUNDATIONS, FUNNY BUSINESS & MURDER

A Stacie Maroni Mystery #2

CHRISTA NARDI

Copyright © 2018 Christa Nardi
All rights reserved.
ISBN: 9781720193470

This is a work of fiction. Although some of the locations may be real, others are fictitious. None of these events actually occurred. All characters are the product of the author's imagination. Any resemblance to real people is entirely coincidental.

Cover Design by Novak Illustrations

Stacie Maroni Mysteries
Prestige, Privilege & Murder (A Stacie Maroni Mystery #1)
Foundations, Funny Business & Murder (A Stacie Maroni Mystery #2)
Deception, Denial & Funny Business (A Stacie Maroni Mystery #3)
Holidays, Hijinks & Murder (A Stacie Maroni Holiday Mystery)
Coming in 2020

Praise for the first Stacie Maroni Mystery, *Prestige, Privilege & Murder*

"I really enjoyed the characters in this story. It has twists and turns and an ending that was a surprise."

"The mystery was enjoyable. The main character, Stacie was very believable and her friends and potential love interest were shaping up to be interesting as well."

CHAPTER 1

For me, the whole point of yoga was to clear my head. As I exited the Yoga Pod, I looked up at the sky and exhaled another cleansing breath. I was lost in the moment when a man barreled into me. The next thing I knew I was on my butt.

"What?" I looked up at a tall man, with an athletic build, black hair, and piercing blue eyes.

"I'm sorry. So sorry." He extended his hands and easily pulled me up, gym bag and all. "Are you all right?"

I nodded.

"I don't usually tackle beautiful women." He scanned the street and with a cryptic "Another time, another place," he ran off.

As if I would know what he was running from or to, I looked up and down the street. Nothing jumped out at me. My cell phone buzzed and I groaned.

"Good morning, Senator."

"Good morning, Stacie. We have a situation here, and I've called a meeting of the Foundation for this evening, six sharp."

So much for my fleeting experience of a clear head. "What kind of situation?"

"I don't want to discuss it on the phone or with each member of the Board individually. Be here at 6 o'clock and you'll find out with the others."

He disconnected. Nothing I could do about it. I tried for another cleansing breath.

The Theodore Noth Foundation was funded by my deceased husband's life insurance policy. The half-million dollars created the foundation to prevent and address domestic violence, one of Ted's and my passions.

Senator William Langford was designated to head up the foundation. He'd pioneered a bill on domestic violence and worked with the NFL and other groups to address the rising concerns.

I walked to my car, parked a block away from the Yoga Pod, and groaned. All the stretches and cleansing breaths weren't going to fix the flat tire. Opting for the positive spin, that made for three downers, so I figured I'd be good for a while.

I called the auto club and walked over to the Starbucks for a Skinny Mocha while I waited. A quick glance at my watch and I placed a call to the office to let Rosie know I had car trouble and would likely be late to work.

Drinking my coffee, I thought about the Senator's call. The board consisted of a myriad of people, including some with deep pockets who, like Ted, were entrepreneurial and could embrace the cause because it cut close to home.

Someone I'd yet to meet represented the sports industry and Langford's connections to the NFL. At the other extreme, the grass roots contingent included the first responders for medical services and police, victims and survivors of domestic violence, and others who worked with the victims, including me.

So far all we'd accomplished was reviewing Ted's requests and instructions, which specified the stakeholders he wanted represented on the board. Langford or his staff drafted a constitution and bylaws. Legal counsel had been retained and an administrative assistant was hired to serve as a combined secretary and treasurer.

I'd yet to meet them or see a final list of the board members. The last communication surrounded a draft announcement for potential grants directed at service and education. How could there be an "emergency" at this point?

My reverie was cut short when the tow truck from the auto club arrived. I joined the mechanic as he examined the tire and shook his head.

"You the owner?"

I nodded and handed him my auto club card.

"You call the police yet?"

"Excuse me. Why would I call the police for a flat tire? I probably drove over a nail or something."

"No, ma'am. This tire has been slashed. You need to make that call. And pop the trunk so I can get out your spare. You have one, right?"

"Slashed?"

"Yes, ma'am." He glanced at the phone in my hand and must have noticed I was in "contacts" as he offered, "Police is 9-1-1. Then you can call whoever else."

I'd actually considered calling a specific policeman. I decided the mechanic's idea was better though and placed the call. With my luck, Officer Rick Murdock would be the responding officer.

We'd dated a few times and I liked Rick. Under different circumstances, it might have worked out. I just wasn't ready for serious and he was. I hadn't heard from him since I said the dreaded "Let's be friends."

The mechanic, "Gordon" from the name on his shirt, pointed to the trunk. I opened it for him and groaned. Seeing the contents, he rolled his eyes. He was nice enough to help me move everything to the back seat.

We'd found the jack and spare when the cruiser pulled up. I released the breath I was holding when Officer Marina Napoli got out, Officer Tim Reardon behind her.

"Hi, Stacie. What's the problem?"

"I came back to my car and had a flat. Gordon here says the tire's been slashed."

"Okay. Reardon, can you check and see if that's been a problem around here lately?" She turned back to me as Reardon walked to the front of my car. Pointing to my coffee cup, Marina asked, "Did you happen to see anyone from the Starbucks?"

I shook my head. "Starbucks came after I called the auto club. I was at the Yoga Pod around the corner."

Reardon joined us and cleared his throat. "No other reports. The sergeant said it was still early. He'll keep us posted if any more reports come in."

With Gordon's help, Reardon took a picture of the slash for the report, while Marina took down the information. Both Gordon and I signed the report, then Gordon got the tire changed.

"Hold on to that tire if you can, just in case something comes up. We'll probably never find out who did this. No cameras and no one called it in if they witnessed it."

Marina shrugged and turned to leave. She turned around and added, "Remember Officer Flatt? He's retiring the end of the month. Send off at the Brick on Friday if you and your friends are interested."

"Thanks, Marina. Maybe I'll see you there."

Gordon stared for a minute, his mouth open. Recovering, he handed me his clipboard to sign. I hoped that was the last of my excitement for the day. If only.

CHAPTER 2

The office building where Senator Langford had his offices was in Reston, about 30 minutes from my townhouse. I'd managed to get home, let Jasper out and feed him, before I pushed the speed limit to be on time for the meeting. I pulled into the parking garage and snagged a spot near the elevator.

Exiting my car, I checked my surroundings and spotted Shawna Jackson. A victim of domestic violence, Shawna was a survivor and managed the Cornerstone Community Women's Shelter. I volunteered there on the weekends to provide trauma counseling. It was comforting to have a personal connection with at least two members of the board, Shawna one of them.

"Stacie, do you know what this meeting is about?"

"No clue. How are you doing? Busy?"

"Not so much. No newcomers since you came by Saturday."

I was about to answer when the elevator opened. We both shrieked at the sight of a body on the floor. The doors were about to close so I stuck my briefcase in the way. I stepped in to check for a pulse while Shawna blocked the door.

"Faint pulse, he's barely breathing."

The elevator alarm went off. While I tried to figure out how to shut off the elevator without touching anything, Shawna called the police. I used a pen to flip the emergency stop switch and the alarm stopped.

A man barreled toward us and the elevator. He wore a suit with a formal, professional air. I recognized him from our one and only meeting of the board two months ago. Stress or whatever, I couldn't remember his name.

"Langford said 6 o'clock sharp. What are you waiting for?"

As one, Shawna and I looked from him to the man on the floor and back.

"Never mind. I'll take the stairs. The meeting is more important." He jogged for the stairwell. I shrugged and hoped he was in good shape. Langford's office was on the 12th floor.

"Did you recognize him, Shawna?"

"Only because he never made eye contact. Too important for the likes of me. Besides, he had a pretentious name – J. Colton Stewart."

I nodded, remembering his attitude. CEO of an up and coming computer gaming company, he was a past client of Ted's and designated by Ted to be on the Board. His comments prompted me to text Langford and let him know Shawna and I were waiting on the police with an injured man. I checked his pulse again; it was faint, but still there.

My phone buzzed and of course it was Senator Langford. "Senator, as I texted, Shawna and I are in the parking garage. Someone is injured and we are waiting on the police to arrive."

"I got that. If Ned Anderson, the admin we hired shows up, tell him to get up here and I don't care if he has to crawl up the twelve flights. And you make sure to tell the police you and Shawna can sign reports later."

As I listened for the approach of sirens, it occurred to me most people would have left the building at around 5 o'clock.

"Senator, who is the admin? Can you describe him to me? I wasn't involved in that process."

"Stacie, who else would be coming here at this hour? I'm sure he'll be distraught at being late for his first meeting. That should be your first clue." With that he disconnected.

I tilted my head and tried to get a better look at the man on the floor. Mostly, we could see his back and longish brown hair. My phone had been on speaker while I spoke with the Senator and I turned to Shawna. "I think he looks distraught, don't you?"

She snorted. "Could be. Guess we'll know as soon as the nice paramedics and police do their thing."

Sirens announced their arrival. The bustle of emergency personnel displaced us to outside the elevator with a stern "Stay put." Senator Langford or J. Colton Stewart must have said something to the others upstairs. The Reston Chief of Police, Frank Rizzo, joined us a few minutes later. A ripple of tension travelled from one responder to the next as the older, distinguished-looking man was recognized.

"Ladies, what happened here?" His voice was calm and cordial. Of course, for him, this was business as usual.

I shrugged. "Don't really know. Shawna and I walked up to the elevator. When the doors opened, there he was."

He nodded slightly. "You arrived together?"

"Separate cars. We arrived at the same time, for the same meeting."

He nodded again as one of the officers came toward us. They saluted and Chief Rizzo broke the silence. "McDonald, what do we have here?"

"White male, early twenties, assaulted. Paramedics have him stabilized and have completed their initial check. No wallet. No identification. He'll be transported."

My phone buzzed with a text from the Senator asking if the admin had arrived. I called him and put the phone on speaker.

"Stacie, a text would do. Either he's on his way up or not."

"Senator, is the admin a white male in his early twenties?"

"What? Why do you want to know that?"

Chief Rizzo extended his hand and I gave him my phone. "Will, do you have a picture as part of the application for this admin? He may be the victim in the elevator. If you have a picture, can you text the picture and his application?"

"Oh, no. I'll…I'll check. My staffers have all left. Let me see what I can find."

"Thank you, Will. And, Will, whatever your emergency was, it will have to wait. This elevator will not be available for a couple of hours. When these ladies are through with reports here, I'm sending them home."

I caught the smile on Shawna's face and shared her relief. The Chief handed me back my phone.

"If no picture, could someone who was part of the interview process possibly identify him?"

He shrugged. "I don't recall what the process was or who was involved, do you?"

I glanced at Shawna and she shook her head. "Maybe the admin was hired before the rest of us were appointed? Hold on. I think the Senator said his name was Ned Anderson."

Shawna nodded. I plugged his name into Google with Virginia. Unfortunately, Ned Anderson was not an uncommon name. Images helped. An older man, a Black man, a younger man, and more. One of them, maybe. I handed my phone back to Chief Rizzo. He took it and walked toward the paramedics.

"What do you think?" Shawna asked.

"All I could see was longish brown hair. I couldn't see his face. The picture is a white guy, young, maybe in his twenties, with brown hair. The chief is coming back."

"Likely it's him. The paramedics said his nose is broken so it's not definitive. If Langford shares the application, we'll try to contact him to at least eliminate him."

He pulled out his phone and placed a call.

"Langford. Is everyone else accounted for?" He grunted at whatever Langford responded.

"Lionel Smythe?" He paused, listening to Langford.

"They're standing next to me. I think that makes them accounted for. Provide whatever info you have on both Anderson and Smythe, ASAP. I'll direct one of the officers to get it from you as soon as they are through with the elevator."

He huffed and responded to whatever the Senator said with, "Reschedule."

He rolled his eyes as he stuffed the phone back into his pocket. Shawna and I gave our statements to the responding officers. By 8 o'clock, I was home, starved, and stressed. The only bright spot was Jasper. My Maltese was quite content to cuddle with me as I ate my Rocky Road ice cream.

CHAPTER 3

Jillian stopped by my office first thing the next morning. I'd barely gotten my jacket off and shoved my purse in the desk drawer when she tapped on the door. My best friend since college, she worked in a different section at Foster's Insurance Group and it was surprising to see her at my door this early.

"How'd your meeting go? Did you hear about the assault at the Langford Building?"

"The meeting never happened, Jillian. Shawna and I … We're the ones who called in the assault."

She plopped down into the chair, her mouth open.

"I don't know much more other than he was still alive when they transported him and he had no identification."

"Stacie, that's awful. What did you do?"

I shrugged. "We stood around until the police told us we could leave. The Senator wasn't too happy, but Chief Rizzo told him the meeting was cancelled and he'd need to reschedule it. So far, no edicts to attend another meeting."

Jillian shook her head. As she leaned back in her chair and set her jaw, I knew she had something on her mind. The news wasn't the only thing that brought her to my office.

"So, Stacie, what are your plans for the weekend? You can't just sit home all the time. We're worried about you."

"I know. It's just. . . I know it's been almost a year since Ted and I split, six months since he was killed. I tried the dating thing with Rick. He's a nice guy and we had fun. I like him okay, but – I don't know. I don't want to date until I'm ready for more than friends, you know what I mean?"

"That doesn't mean you have to stay home. As for Rick, yeah, he's a nice guy. You don't have to fall in love or marry any 'nice guy' who comes along. You're young, Stacie. And all you do is work, volunteer at Cornerstone and occasionally the animal shelter, and yoga. You're stuck in time. Have you even looked into classes or getting another degree? That was your dream."

I shook my head and studied the floor. "You're right. It was, I don't know, too soon and then it was too late to look into fall semester. If I want to get into the program at George Mason, I need to get everything in by December."

"I can't help you with that, but time isn't standing still."

She sat up and leaned toward me. "Stacie, how about we get a group together and go out Friday night? Not a date, just out with Trina, Wade, and me and whoever else you want to invite? Some place besides Creekview Lounge where you met both Ted and Rick? You know, a change in venue?"

"Hmm. Um. Did I tell you Marina was one of the officers who responded to my slashed tire yesterday?" I knew I didn't. On purpose.

"No. What did she have to say?"

"Do you remember Officer Flatt – older, grumpy man? He was Rick's partner." At her nod, I continued.

"Marina mentioned there's a party at The Brick to celebrate Flatt's retirement. She invited us all."

The Brick was an odd combination of cop and biker bar – a sharp contrast to the Creekview Lounge where the professional singles hung out. I'd never been and Jillian's husband, Wade, hadn't exactly encouraged our going there.

"Huh. Not sure why Marina mentioned it to you. Definitely Rick would be there and that could be awkward. She must realize that. Another option would be Rockies." Rockies was another place to go for dancing, but not as classy as Creekview.

Trina bounded into the room as Jillian responded. The three of us were good friends even before we all ended up working at Foster's Insurance Group. Trina was the wild one of the three of us.

"Did you hear about the party for Flatt this Friday. Bill told me about it last night. We're going."

Trina met Bill, a Beckman Springs police officer, the last time we all went out together. Although she didn't tend to stay with the same guy for very long, they were still dating six months later.

"I don't know, Trina." I shook my head.

"If you're worried about Rick, Bill says he's dating someone now. They're all teasing him about his wanting to get married and have children."

I smiled. "That was the problem. He was at Creekview with every intention of trying to find a wife. He's a good guy. He'll make someone a great husband. Another time in my life, maybe. Not now, not yet."

I'd been reeling after discovering Ted cheated on me, and then he was killed. With the investigation into his murder, I learned just how much he had hidden from me, his wife. I wasn't ready to go down that road again.

"Well, see, now that's not an issue. You could come, hang out with us, and have a good time. I bet that hunk Detective O'Hare will be there, too. He doesn't strike me as the marrying kind and he sure is nice to look at. Don't tell Bill I said that though."

My mouth dropped and Jillian burst out laughing.

"Okay, I'll go. No matchmaking. Not even with the hunk Detective, you hear?"

They both nodded and Jillian stood up as Rosie stuck her head in the door. "We got a situation in contracts. Can you go over there?"

She had the phone message form in her hand. I took it and race walked to the elevator, leaving Rosie and my friends to their own devices. Part of my job at Foster's was crisis intervention. Rosie's message of a "situation" translated into a crisis and one that most often had nothing to do with work. The message came from a project director, Sandy Kovax, and that was where I headed.

On the third floor, I turned and Sandy met me in the hallway. She exhaled and looked behind her and then back at me.

"Stacie, I'm so glad you were available. Kayla Anderson looks like she's been through a war zone – not physically, but emotionally. One of the other team members asked her a question and she started sobbing and then she hyperventilated. I got her to breathe into a bag and took her into my office. Now she's unresponsive."

We'd walked while she talked. As we entered her project area, the other workers scurried to their desks like ants. I heard Sandy groan and saw the brief shake of her head as we continued to her office.

As often before, I wondered whose idea it was for manager offices to have glass walls. It defied the idea of a private office when anyone and everyone could see what was happening. On the other hand, there'd be no hanky-panky in private offices during work hours.

Kayla sat there, brown paper bag in her hand. Young, maybe twenty, she had on slacks and a shirt. The shirt wasn't buttoned correctly. Her eyes were red and puffy, her skin pale. If she'd had any make up on before, it was long gone. I signaled for Sandy to leave and tried to figure the best way to position myself. I knelt down on the floor by the chair and put my hand over hers.

"Kayla, I'm Stacie. Ms. Kovax is concerned about you." At least she looked at me. I continued, "Can you tell me what happened so I can help you?"

"I'm sorry. I'm so sorry." She sobbed and I looked for tissues. Handing her the box, I tried to reassure her.

"We'll figure out what to do. Can you tell me what happened? What you're sorry about?"

Between her sobs, I caught "newlyweds," "pregnant," "scared," and then "He didn't come home last night. I didn't mean to get pregnant."

"Take some deep, slow breaths. Let's try to sort this out. And not jump to conclusions. Have you talked to your husband this morning?"

She shook her head. "I kept waking up and he wasn't there. The phone rang but I didn't answer – caller unknown. I don't know where Ned could be."

I'd been kneeling and I sat my butt down on my feet. "Ned Anderson" was a common name. I'd seen that last night, yet hearing it threw me.

"Kayla, when was the last time you talked to him and where was he going?"

"He had some meeting in Reston. A part-time job to make extra money for the baby…" She started sobbing and then the hiccups set in.

"Slow, deep breaths. I'll see about getting you some water." I stuck my head out the door. "Can someone get a bottle of water for Kayla, please? Thanks."

Sandy came to the door and I took the bottle from her. "Here you go, Kayla. Take a few minutes to calm down, okay."

Walking to the farthest corner, I pulled out my phone and googled the Reston Police Department and hit the call button.

"No, this is not an emergency. Can I be connected with whomever is in charge of the assault last evening at the Langford Building – this is Stacie Maroni, one of the women who called it in."

"I'll transfer you."

"McDonald here."

"Officer McDonald, this is Stacie Maroni from last night. I'm at work and one of the employees, a Mrs. Anderson is concerned her husband Ned hasn't come home." I left it there and hoped he would connect the dots.

He cleared his throat. "We haven't identified the victim as yet. We got no answer when we called the numbers Langford gave us late last night for the missing admin. You think this may be the wife?"

I looked over at her. "Right age. She said he went to a meeting last night in Reston and never came home. She also said she had a couple of calls last night but didn't answer as callerID said 'caller unknown.' Could have been your calls. What now?"

"What's your number and location? I'll check with my boss. I should've been home a few hours ago." He sounded tired. I gave him the information and went back to Kayla.

"Kayla, I think it would be a good idea if you came to my office. We need to check some things and maybe we can find out what happened to Ned. Can you collect your things and come with me?"

She nodded and stood up. Definitely a baby bump. She led me to her cubicle and desk. I nodded to Sandy and said quietly, "Kayla and I are going up to my office. We'll get this sorted out and then I think she should go home. Sick day."

Sandy nodded agreement, and as we were leaving, she touched Kayla's shoulder. "Kayla, you take care of yourself and your baby. Don't worry about anything here. Hopefully, we'll see you tomorrow."

Sandy looked at me for confirmation that I could not give. I rubbed Kayla's back as we made our way back to my office with solid walls and, most of the time, privacy.

CHAPTER 4

The rest of the day was a blur. In my office, I asked some more questions, trying for a conversational tone. "Kayla, that meeting Ned was supposed to go to last night? Did he mention who he was meeting with?"

Her eyebrows knitted, she answered, "Lang something."

"Ahh. Just so you know, I've called the police to see if perhaps they have any information on Ned's whereabouts. They'll want to talk to you. Do you have a picture of Ned with you?"

"Police? Is Ned okay? Yes, I have a picture." She dug into her bag and pulled out her wallet and a picture from their wedding. The photographer caught their happiness and optimism and love in that picture.

"I don't know the answer to that question. But take a deep breath and we'll find out. Is there anyone – a family member you'd like to call? Your doctor maybe?"

She didn't have a chance to answer before Rosie let me know the Reston police arrived. I asked Rosie to alert any officers coming to talk with Kayla that she was pregnant and distressed and told her to show them to my office. I managed to get the doctor's information and her sister's information before the officers arrived at my door.

The female officer, Bristol, immediately sat down next to Kayla and got as much information for the report as she could, as well as Ned's photo. The other officer, Firestone, took down my information. Catching the expression between them, I knew what was coming before Bristol spoke.

"Kayla, we think your husband may have been mugged last night. A man meeting his description was found at the Langford Building in Reston. He had no identification on him and his wallet was gone."

"But surely he can tell you who he is or if it's Ned, he could call me. Wait, does this man have amnesia?"

I stepped a little closer and placed my hand on Kayla's shoulder in anticipation.

"I'm sorry, this man didn't regain consciousness. We'll need someone…"

"Noooooo! Nooooo!" She started sobbing and hyperventilating. I got her a bag to breath into as I directed my attention to the officers. "You calling for the paramedics or am I?"

Bristol nodded and I handed her the information on Kayla's ObGyn. I continued to prompt Kayla to breath slowly and deeply. She muttered. All I could catch was "mistake," "Ned," and a few other words. I mentioned the name of the closest hospital and she nodded. Firestone suggested another hospital – the one they'd taken Ned to – but she shook her head. He looked like he was going to insist.

"Officer, first priority here is with this mother and her baby. Identification can wait and may have to be done by someone else."

He opened his mouth to argue with me and Bristol spoke up. "She's right. We're done here." She stood up and handed me her card as I heard noise in the hallway. The paramedic team had arrived and, after confirming with Kayla, I stepped out into the hallway and called her sister.

"Ms. Boles? This is Stacie Maroni from Foster's where your sister works. She gave me your phone number."

"Is she okay? What's wrong?"

"She's been very upset today and the paramedics are checking her now to make sure she and the baby are okay. They'll be transporting her to Independence Medical as a precaution."

"What? I don't understand. I mean I know pregnancy emotions are crazy… Can I speak with my sister?"

"I think so. Hold on."

They had Kayla on the stretcher in the hall by then.

"Kayla, your sister wants to talk to you." I extended the phone, ignoring the grimace of the paramedic. She took the phone and said her sister's name. Then her husband's name and the sobbing began again.

I took the phone away from her and the paramedics escaped any further interruption after shaking their head at me. Back on the phone, I caught her sister mid-sentence.

"…understand. What about Ned? Did something happen to him?"

"This is Stacie again. Kayla is on the way to the hospital. It has not yet been confirmed. Ned may have been mugged and died as a result. The police need someone to do the identification before it is official though."

"Oh my gosh! I'll... Maybe it's not him. Maybe it's a mistake ... It's not a mistake, is it?"

"No, ma'am. I'm afraid not. I have the police officer's information. Can you help your sister find someone else to do the identification?"

"Of course. I... I'll make some calls and then go to the hospital."

I gave her the officer's information and we disconnected. I looked up to find Sandy at my door. Rosie must have let her know when the paramedics arrived.

"She was assaulted. She's pregnant and he assaulted her?"

Most of the time, that is when either Lynisha, my co-worker, or I call for an ambulance, so her assumption wasn't completely off kilter. Domestic violence is more common than one would think.

"No, Sandy. She wasn't assaulted. It's not confirmed, but very likely Ned's the one who was assaulted last night at the Langford Building. He didn't make it."

She gasped and I continued. "Hospital for Kayla? Precautionary measure."

Sandy's anger dissolved and she stood there with her mouth open. "What can we do?"

I shrugged. "I'll let you know when I know more. Likely she or her sister or someone will notify you. I'm sure it will be on the news as well."

Sandy tried for a smile and left. I closed my door and put my head down. Exhausted. Drained.

I'd barely gotten into my work groove when Jillian, Trina, and Ronnie showed up. Lunchtime already. Ronnie was a new addition to our group and to Foster's. She'd worked for Ted before he was killed. In the aftermath, we'd become friends.

Of course, the excitement of the morning was the major topic. Ronnie shared pictures of Elle and sang her praises. Trina almost seemed wistful as she looked at the little girl, once again surprising me. I thought I'd escaped the inevitable when Ronnie brought up my future plans.

"Stacie, you haven't talked much about going back to school." She shrugged. "You have a knack for working with people in stress and I can tell you really care. You're a generous person. Isn't that what you talked about doing?"

"Umm. Yes. I'm just not ready. And honestly, sometimes the thought of all day, every day, dealing with crises and victims? I'm not sure."

Jillian nodded and grinned. "Something to be said for your job here at Foster's. You get the adrenalin rush every so often to break up the predictable – and I'm guessing here – boring tables and actuarial charts. You could still get the degree and be better able to handle the crisis and mental health stuff without doing it full-time, you know."

"I'm still a work in progress. I've realized that my resentment of Ted and his family not wanting – not allowing – me to pursue graduate school was more me fighting against the control thing than the graduate education thing, if you follow me."
Needless to say, my three independent thinking friends all agreed.

CHAPTER 5

Though I don't usually watch the evening news, I made it a point to turn on the television before I fed Jasper and scrounged in my refrigerator to throw together something resembling dinner. I was eating my naked burger and salad when the newscaster got my attention.

"Update on the mugging at the Langford Building last evening. The mugging victim, Mr. Ned Anderson, did not regain consciousness. Reston Police ask anyone with information that could help identify the person or persons responsible to contact them." They showed the wedding picture of Ned and Kayla.

The other newscaster continued, "He reportedly was at the Langford Building for a meeting of the Theodore Noth Foundation, a foundation, ironically enough, that aims to prevent and provide support for victims of violence. In response to the incident, Senator Langford, the appointed Chairman to the Foundation Board, reiterated the importance of the foundation given the rise in violent crimes. No one has spoken to J. Colton Stewart or Stacie Maroni Noth for their comments on Anderson's death."

I jumped up and screamed, startling Jasper. "No! You got it all wrong!" Not surprisingly, my phone immediately buzzed and rang.

"Hello, Senator."

"Did you see the news? Good coverage for the Foundation, don't you think?"

"No. I don't think. The Foundation is specific to domestic violence. There is no indication that Ned Anderson was a victim of domestic violence and your statement implied he was. It also has nothing to do with the rise in violent crime."

"Now, you listen here. This was a mugging and I'm sorry the young man died. Any publicity is good publicity as long as we are seen as fighting against violence."

"I disagree, Senator. Should they ask me for a statement, I will clarify the mission for the Foundation is specific to domestic violence and there's no indication that's what happened to Ned Anderson. His family deserves that. And how did they get my name and J. Colton Stewart's?" I didn't bother to point out they got my name wrong.

"No idea. Must be from the incorporation papers. Or Trichter or Smythe."

"Who is Smythe?" Trichter was Ted's attorney and executor of his estate, but other than mention of his name by Chief Rizzo, I had no clue who Smythe was.

"He's legal counsel for the foundation. He'll be calling you – and everyone else on the board – in the next few days. He's trying to figure out what Anderson was all in a tither about."

"So, you don't know?"

"He said something about the incorporation paperwork and by-laws and who was or wasn't on the Board. It seemed best to let him explain it all as I couldn't make much sense of it. As soon as I get another admin hired, I'll notify everyone of a meeting and we'll get to the bottom of this. Good night, Stacie."

He disconnected. Irritated, I replied to the dead air, "Good night, Will."

I shook my head and pulled up my texts as I sat down to finish my dinner.

The text from Jillian was short. "Heads up – you were mentioned on the news in connection with Ned Anderson."

The text from my attorney and close family friend, Nate, was equally as short and to the point. "You and the foundation were just on the news."

I stared at my phone in anticipation of the dreaded, but inevitable, call from Hamilton Noth, Ted's father. It occurred to me, he would be most pleased with the omission of domestic violence from the description. That irked me to no end.

The paperwork and reports to sift through demanded my attention and energy. No new crises meant I got almost caught up with last month's month end reports. The funeral for Ned was scheduled for Thursday and I planned to go. The more I thought about it, the more I agreed with the conclusion that he was mugged and it had nothing to do with the foundation.

I hoped the senator added security to his building for any after-hours meetings in the future. Two days and no word from Langford to reschedule was odd. I did get a phone call from Lionel Smythe though.

"Ms. Maroni or is it Noth? This is Lionel Smythe. I am the legal counsel retained by the Noth Foundation."

"Hello, Mr. Smythe. It's Maroni and that's the Theodore Noth Foundation. What can I do for you?"

"No offense intended, Ms. Maroni." He cleared his throat. "I've been asked to contact each of the members of the Foundation Executive Board in light of the murder of Ned Anderson."

"What exactly are you contacting us about?" It didn't make sense to me given the police had all our reports.

"Apparently, there is no physical record of the hiring process. Do you have any idea who was involved in that process? Who interviewed him? Who made the hiring decision?"

I chuckled. "No more than I know what process was used to retain you. Is there any paper trail on that?" I heard the intake of breath and had to smile, imagining his jaw drop.

"I . . . I don't really know the answer to that question."

"So, Mr. Smythe, how did you come to be legal counsel? My impression was Senator Langford handled all that, which most likely means his staffers handled it. Now in your case, maybe you had mutual friends or he or his staffers looked for lawyers with experience in foundation related or non-profit areas. An admin? Not sure. From my conversations with his widow, she didn't even know Langford was a senator, so no personal connections there."

Dead silence before he responded.

"One of his staffers contacted me. I did not previously have any contact with Senator Langford. Honestly, my only contact thus far has been via telephone. As you alluded, I do serve as legal counsel for many non-profits in DC, Maryland, and Virginia. I was provided with a copy of the constitution, bylaws, mission of the Theodore Noth Foundation, and the names of members of the Executive Board – none of whom I've ever met. The two senators, Police Chief Rizzo and Fire Chief Petkra – I know of them obviously. I also was given the contact information for Mr. Trichter. Does that answer your question?"

"Yes, sir. It does. I would guess Ned was hired in the same way. Perhaps you can answer another question. We were all supposed to be at the Langford Building for a meeting that night, yourself included, for an emergency situation. What was the emergency? The foundation hasn't done anything yet."

"Uh… That's one of the curious things. Mr. Anderson was the one who asked the meeting be called. He indicated that the records he received raised some questions that needed to be addressed by the board. Some issues with the filing of the foundation paperwork and something about the bank account. If he shared those concerns with the senator, the senator is not sharing."

"And is someone else looking at those same records to see what might have triggered his request for the meeting and potentially his death?"

"Now, Ms. Maroni, it is sad the man died, but clearly this was a random mugging and nothing connected to the foundation or board. Senator Langford indicated the records were reviewed and nothing was found. My office is checking on the paperwork related to the foundation filing and what might have caught Mr. Anderson's eye."

I wondered how often random muggings occurred at the Langford building. Was it just a coincidence a mugging occurred at the same time as a meeting called by the victim? On the other hand, I knew nothing about what was required to become a non-profit foundation. I'd seen a draft of the articles of incorporation, bylaws, and who might be on the Board. Then my conflict of interest statement to be signed.

"Mr. Smythe, has it occurred to you that if the records came from Senator Langford's staffers and they are the ones looking over them, they could miss what someone else seeing the same papers for the first time would catch? As legal counsel, don't you think an external audit or review of all the records, financial and otherwise, might be appropriate."

"As you yourself noted, no monies have been disbursed. What would there be to look at?"

"Maybe that's the issue. Especially if he mentioned the bank account. A red flag if monies were disbursed with no paper trail? And I'm guessing monies were disbursed to cover your retainer? And to cover filing fees for incorporation and whatever else?"

"Hmm. I'll give that consideration. With your suspicious nature, maybe you should consider law. I'm not sure what the next steps will be, aside from hiring a new admin. I have the rest of this list of board members to speak with yet. Thank you for your cooperation."

We disconnected and I reflected on the conversation. Me, go into law? Heaven forbid. What he'd shared made little sense to me. Who hired people in this day and age of being sued or accused of discrimination without a paper trail? As HR at Foster's, I kept all the paperwork on when a position was posted, what the requirements were, who applied, who was interviewed and by whom, and the criteria for selection. Very detailed records, my specialty, or as Jillian' husband, Wade, often teased, my obsessive-compulsive tendency.

Even the selection of board members should have had some rationale and a clear-cut process to ensure there was no apparent bias. Langford had probably delegated the process to his staffers. I'd never given much thought to all the people in politicians' offices. Just more reasons to stay away from politics and law.

While all this swirled through my brain, I made dents in all the piles and reports, leaving a little later than usual. I couldn't dilly dally with Jasper waiting on me, yet that didn't stop me from ruminating over all the errands I needed to run or chores that needed to be done.

As a result, I paid little attention to my surroundings as I exited the building into the parking lot. Once outside the door, I was surprised to see a car pull up next to where my car was parked and a man step out. A shiver went down my spine when I saw the way he looked around and then scrutinized my car.

Training on how not to be a victim kicked in and I immediately pressed the panic button on my key fob and ducked behind the nearest car. Phone out, I called 9-1-1 as I heard the other car peel out. Only then did I stop the blaring alarm. One of the custodians ran out the door behind me and stayed with me until Napoli and Reardon showed up.

"You making this a habit, Stacie? No flat this time. What happened?"

"I was coming out of the building and a car pulled into the space next to my car. A man got out and looked around. I was back here and he must not have seen me. He nodded to whoever was driving. He had something in his hand and started toward my car. He looked like he was doing something to the car. I hit the panic button and they took off."

"Driver side?" I nodded to Reardon and he jogged over to my car.

Napoli looked to the custodian. "ID please. And can you tell me what you saw or heard?"

"I heard the alarm and came running. I found Ms. Maroni here shaking and saw that sports car burn rubber. He couldn't get out of here fast enough."

"He? So it was a man driving? You saw him?"

"No, I couldn't see the driver. Doesn't change anything. A man was driving that car to handle it how he did." He nodded his head for emphasis.

"Okay. Thank you. Stacie, …"

"Found this on the undercarriage." Reardon held up a small plastic bag with what looked like a metal disk. Sensing my confusion, he elaborated. "Tracking device. Somebody wants to know exactly where you are all the time."

I sucked in a deep breath and leaned against the closest car. Speechless, I shook my head.

"Okay. Now we know the immediate intent. Plant the tracking device. Stacie, can you describe the car or the man who got out of the car?"

"White male, average height, average weight. Nothing stood out. The car was flashy – red and black. Maybe a Mazda Miata or Fiat? Can you trace that thing?"

The custodian nodded to my description of the car. "New model, too."

Reardon shrugged in response to my question about the tracker.

"Anyone stalking you? Unwanted advances?"
I shook my head. Napoli handed me the clipboard to sign the report. "We'll let you know if we find out anything. Keep your eyes open, Stacie."

CHAPTER 6

There was no real reason for me to go to Ned's funeral. My rationalization was that somehow Ted's foundation caused him to, if nothing else, be in that building that night. And then, there was Kayla, and my curiosity. So, I donned my almost too short go-to-funeral dress and went.

I was pleasantly surprised to see Sandy and a few other of Kayla's co-workers there. They gave me reasonable credibility for being there as well. More surprising, given that the funeral was in Beckman Springs, Officer McDonald of Reston PD was present as was an unfamiliar Beckman Springs Officer. For a mugging, even a fatal one, that seemed unusual. McDonald nodded to me from where the two of them stood.

Thankfully, it was a short service. I didn't plan on going to the cemetery or the repast for the family. I paid my respects to Kayla and her family members and prepared to leave.

Bells went off in my head when I spotted O'Hare leaning against my car. He had been the detective in charge of the investigation of Ted's murder. He wore what was apparently his one and only sports jacket. No matter. As Trina pointed out, he looked good.

"Stacie. Nice dress."

I flashed back to his comment on my dress being a distraction after Ted's funeral. Various emotions flitted through me and I ended on confusion.

"What? Why are you here?"

He snickered. "You seem to be coming up a lot this week. You're a busy lady." He paused and when I didn't volunteer any information, he continued.

"Monday someone slashes your tire and later that evening, you report a crime – the murder of a young man in Reston. The young man being buried today. Then yesterday, someone tries to put a tracking device on your car."

He hesitated and shook his head. "The one piece of paper the killer didn't take is an email that includes your name in the text – McDonald of Reston PD advised my officer of that during the service. And now, here we are."

"That about sums up my week, Detective. Unfortunately, I have no explanation for any of it. And I didn't know about the email you mentioned."

"It was about the foundation, to Senator Langford from Mr. Anderson, and stated the only record he could find of legitimate members of the Board were the Senator, you, and someone named Stewart."

I nodded. That must be where the newscaster got our names.

He exhaled a deep, audible breath. "While you're in Beckman Springs, anything look off? You call us. Reston PD isn't buying a random mugging. The two other incidents with you in as few days don't jibe with that either. Use that fancy alarm system, Stacie. And you might consider not driving yourself places – Uber or taxi or carpool. Something's not right."

He walked away. Numb, I got in my car. Glad I had a gym bag with me, I detoured to the Yoga Pod before going to work. The afternoon was uneventful. At home, I took Jasper for a quick walk and cuddled with him. Maybe not certified, but Jasper was my therapy dog.

I connected with my friend Google to learn about tracking devices and how to detect them. I ordered a small electronic sweeper advertised on the website. It may not be as effective as promised, but it made me feel better. I'd gotten into bed when I remembered the alarm system. Up again, I let Jasper out one last time, checked all the doors, and armed the system.

The week had sailed by and with it my dread of the retirement gig at the Brick only worsened. Waiting for Wade and Jillian, my father called. It was good to talk to him, even if he did nag.

"Hi, Dad. How are you?"

"I'm good, Stacie, really good. But I'm a father and I'm concerned about you."

"I'm good. Honest."

"You're getting out, going places? I can't say I wasn't elated when you stopped seeing the cop, yet at least you weren't sitting at home like an old lady."

"No, I'm not that old yet. Jillian and the gang – we're all going out tonight. To a cop bar for a retirement send off." I chuckled to myself, sure he cringed.

"Okay, at least you're getting out. Must be other people going to that bar besides cops, right?"

"Well, yeah. It's also a biker bar." I knew it was mean, but I couldn't resist.

"You're killing me, Stacie. I have news for you though."

"Yeah?"

"You've met Deanna and you know I've been spending more time upstate. She's agreed to marry me."

"That's great, Dad. I'm happy for you." He'd been lonely since my mother died so many years ago and, although initially surprised when he started seeing someone, I knew this was good for him. Besides, I liked Deanna.

"It will be a small affair. You'll come to the wedding?"

"Of course. Have you set a date? Does Nate know yet?"

Nate and my dad went way back and Nate still advised me on legal matters like my divorce that never happened, from time to time. Last time my dad came down to see me, he spent as much time or more with Nate as me. I suspected back then Nate was helping him with a prenup.

"No date yet. We may wait until after the new year – early January. As for Nate, he's the next call on my list."

"Let me know when you have the date set. And congratulations to you both. Wade and Jillian pulled into the drive, so I have to go."

I didn't use the security system my dad had installed after Ted's murder as much as I probably should, but I did like the video of my driveway so I could tell who arrived and when. I set the alarm, grabbed my purse, and plastered a smile on my face.

CHAPTER 7

Never having been to the Brick before, I studied the building and tilted my head to try and get it to be level. Not happening. The Brick was an old wood frame structure with stone and brick in what seemed like random places and either it was built to be lopsided or one side was sinking. It reminded me of the saloons in old westerns, but with real doors. Not a lot of windows though.

Originally a biker bar, motorcycle cops had infiltrated and now they shared the location without any conflicts, and perhaps even some respect. For me, the best part of The Brick was I didn't have to pretend to be someone I'm not. The Brick was definitely low on the pretentious scale. I could be middle class me. Jeans, a sweater, and boots were all I had to worry about. Everything color-coordinated and comfortable.

We spotted Trina even in the subdued lighting that hid who knew what. As always, she dressed in bright colors, with her hair tinted in stripes to match. She flitted around the table and Bill without ever truly sitting down. She reminded me of a Monarch butterfly.

"About time you got here! Do you all know each other?" she asked as she assaulted us with hugs.

After the round of introductions to cover the few people in her group we didn't know, Wade went to the bar to get our drinks. No Viognier tonight – the wine selections were limited. The beer offerings, on the other hand, ranged from traditional brands to craft beers, on tap or by the bottle.

I smiled and made small talk while I checked out the place. It was a mixed crowd, mostly dressed like me in jeans and, other than Trina, in more subdued tones. A few wore leather vests, but not many. A few Harley-Davidson jackets or tee-shirts. Flatt and some other guys gathered not far from us, under one of the large screens that offered additional light to the area than the lights themselves. I didn't see Rick and realized I had mixed emotions – relief and disappointment.

I smiled at some comment and then the screen grabbed my attention. A talk show, from what I could tell, with an interviewee who looked like the guy who knocked me down earlier in the week. Someone tapped my shoulder and I turned, smile in place.

"Hi, Stacie. How are you, today?"

I wondered if Trina was behind the good detective's sudden appearance or if it was business.

"Detective O'Hare, nice to see you again. I'm doing fine. And you?"

He smiled and waved his arm around the room for effect. "Stacie, within these walls, here? It's Michael. The titles get left at the door and hopefully the job, too."

"Okay…Michael." A little uncomfortable. At a loss for words, I glanced at the screen, the interview continuing. "Do you know who that is by any chance?"

He frowned as he watched the screen for a few seconds. "The woman is Barbie Blake. She does a talk show. This must be a pre-game clip or a delayed game clip. Usually they show sports not talk shows here."

"But who is she interviewing? He looks familiar but I don't know who he is?"

"Oh, not into sports much, huh?"

I shrugged. It was no big deal. I jumped when all of a sudden Elvis and "Fools Rush In" blared. He laughed.

"Jukebox. Very old jukebox. Care to dance?"

I looked around and sure enough there were people dancing. I put down my drink.

"Sure." After all, what could it hurt? Maybe my friends would get off my back at least. Besides, it turned out he wasn't a bad dancer.

The music stopped and he smiled. "Thanks. Want anything from the bar?"

I shook my head. One not so great white wine could last a long time. I turned and stopped. Rick was over with my friends. With trepidation, I pasted the smile back on and joined the group.

"… new partner at the end of the month. Instead of being the junior guy, I may even be top dog."

Bill, Trina's beau, chuckled. "Yeah, right." He glanced around before he asked, "O'Hare give you a heads up?"

Rick shook his head and turned in my direction. "Hi Stacie. You staying out of trouble?"

"Trying. How are you doing?"

"Good." The petite woman standing near him turned and nudged him.

"Right. Stacie, you were dancing when we got here. Stacie, I'd like you to meet Maria. Maria, this is Stacie Maroni."

"Hi Maria. Nice to meet you."

She nodded in return.

Wade swore and we all turned to him. "That woman – well most of these talk show people – they invite you on the show and you think great exposure, and then they twist it. I don't know what she just said. His smile faded and he stiffened up. I'll have to catch this clip sometime when I can hear what they're saying. Time for another beer."

I looked to Jillian and tried to telegraph the question "Did he do that to get the focus off Rick, Maria, and me or does he really care that much?" Although I couldn't tell if she really understood the question, she caught that I questioned his outburst and shrugged.

Trina grabbed both of us as the jukebox blared "Beautiful Noise" and although the last thing I wanted to do was dance again, it offered escape.

Thankfully, Rick and Maria had moved to the group with Flatt when the music ended. We saw Marina and some of the others we knew. I kept smiling and making small talk, a skill I'd worked on as Ted's wife with stuffy parties and surface level relationships.

I still wanted to ask about Wade's comment and if he could tell me anything about the man. The opportunity came on the drive home.

"So, Wade, did you come up with all that about talk show hosts as a distraction or do you really have these deep-seated feelings I've never heard about before?"

He chuckled. "A little of both. Not much interested in conversation at the table, I'd been tracking the interchange. I am curious what she said or asked that got him riled. I do think it was a set up and no one deserves that."

Maybe because he worked in security or as a Black man had been treated badly, Wade often was a bit suspicious and cynical. I didn't get a chance to ask about the man again though because Jillian shifted the conversation.

"That wasn't so bad, Stacie, was it? You got to dance and hang out and no pressure, right?" Jillian was making a point and I nodded.

"Maybe next time we can go to Rockies. What do you think?"

"I haven't been there in ages. For sure, it's not as dark and the wine was at least better. I know. Do you know if anyone is having a charity event casino night? That's social but with something to do. Fall's usually a big time for them."

"That's a great idea." Jillian beamed. Wade nodded his agreement. Now, we just had to find one that didn't require big bucks to partake.

CHAPTER 8

My phone rang way too early the next morning. CallerID told me it was Nate, and I smiled. He probably wanted to talk about dad and the wedding. Make sure I was okay with it.

"Morning, Nate. You do know it is early for some of us...."

"I caught the local 'good morning' show and they were talking sports and violence and reported on some basketball player who's part of a non-profit for personal gain. Stacie, they named Ted's Foundation."

"Huh? I don't know that there's even a basketball player on the Board. And what is the personal gain?"

"I'm not sure. What I caught was two people talking about something on another show. I wasn't paying attention so I didn't catch the whole thing. What do you know?"

"Not much. There was some issue, possibly legal, and we were supposed to meet. You know about the mugging at the Langford Building. The meeting was supposed to be there and with the mugging, the meeting got cancelled.

Nate, do you know anything about Lionel Smythe? He was retained as Foundation legal counsel."

"No, but I'll see what I can find out and if I hear anything else, I'll let you know. Be careful, Stacie, someone could get hurt here."

We disconnected. Nate was right. If something was not cricket with the Foundation, someone would become the scape goat, and the Senators, Chief of Police and Fire, and others with money and position, would not be the targets. And, obviously, someone had already gotten hurt.

I should have anticipated the next call from my dad. Nate had alerted him to this new wrinkle with the foundation.

"You be sure to document everything and have witnesses, Stacie, you hear? People are always looking for someone to blame."

"Yes, Dad. I hear you. The foundation hasn't even had its first meeting yet and there's a lawyer checking everything."

"Okay, and Stacie, you're using that security system, right? I've had a bad feeling all along about your involvement with this foundation. It would be better if you had a clear break from everything to do with that Noth family."

He had a point. "I know Dad. Only the foundation mission to address domestic violence aligns with what I think I want to do with my life – working with the victims."

"So, have you decided what you're going to do? How you're going to use the monies from Ted?"

I hesitated. My inheritance provided me with the funds to pursue my graduate education – to take back what marrying Ted and his family's values on the role of women had blocked. "Not exactly. Right now they're in short term investment while I figure things out."

"Whatever you decide, know I'll support you. I've gotta run. Stay safe."

It was earlier than I'd have liked, but Jasper was wide awake and bouncing in circles to go out. I cleaned up a little, played with Jasper, and even turned on the television to see if there was a talk show I could catch. Not my favorite choice of shows and it became easily ignored background noise. Next stop, Cornerstone Community Women's Shelter.

Thinking over Nate's call as I drove, I remembered the name of the representative from the Sports Commission and had to laugh despite myself. The name Austin Beasley seemed more fitting for a nobleman or butler than a football player. In my head, football players were rough and physical – and their names should fit. Who knows? Maybe Austin Beasley played football to prove he was rough and tough, unlike his name. Still, he played football, not basketball.

I arrived at Cornerstone and Shawna greeted me, the stress lines in her face more evident than usual.

"So glad you're here, Stacie. It's been a week." I gave her a hug. Shawna was a survivor and had seen a lot both personally and since taking on the direction of Cornerstone. We moved into the office area and I grabbed a cup of coffee.

"The hot-line got a call and an address and not much else. Layla checked it out. There were two young girls, maybe in their teens, in bad shape. Possibly caught up in human trafficking. They're still too scared to talk yet. The area wasn't safe and Layla brought them here. Police were notified and came. Dr. Hanreddy checked and took care of the medical side. We all agree they're underage but no ID and no confirmation. Bad shape – physically and emotionally."

"Any change since they've been here?" Hopefully, they would get the message they were safe, open up and tell their story.

"No. One of them, we're calling her Princess Vi, sleeps most of the time. She has the worst injuries, and has had IV antibiotics, blood, you name it. Dr. Hanreddy is with her now. We're trying to avoid hospitalizing her – afraid it could be traumatic and possibly place her in danger. The other one, Princess Why, hasn't said anything except 'why.' She has a broken leg and ribs. She's alert and looks around. She's taking it in. If one of the other women approaches her though, she recoils."

I shook my head. Dr. Hanreddy joined us. She shook her head and poured herself a cup.

"Hi, Stacie. Bad week for the good guys. I replaced the IVs and Princess Vi is getting stronger. Blood work will tell us for sure if we're on the right track here. Shawna, you know the drill. Be careful with any organic waste – we don't know what this child has been exposed to. Her pain level seems to have lessened so I've cut the sedation. Hopefully, she'll be more alert over the next few days. Let me know… well, you know the drill."

"What about the other girl?" I asked.

"Physically? She's on the mend." She shrugged. "Her vitals are good. Some good food and a safe haven? Maybe in a few more days she might say something."

Dr. Hanreddy chuckled. "When she said 'why' just now, I asked her 'why not?' She at least reacted and made eye contact. First time."

"Probably didn't realize anyone was listening or hearing her. We'll make a point to answer in some way if she verbalizes or makes a sound." Shawna made a note for the bulletin board so everyone would know.

"Everyone else?"

"Two of them were asking for you, Stacie." Dr. Hanreddy indicated on the chart which ones and I nodded. That's where I'd start.

"Anything else happening here?"

"Not really, Stacie. Sorry I missed you ladies the other night. The senator was beside himself that everyone didn't jump at his request. And pretty nervous, too." Dr. Hanreddy grimaced.

"Did he say anything about what the meeting was about?"

"No, and then the lawyer called to ask questions. Did he call you, too?"

Shawna and I both nodded. On a whim, I asked, "Did you hear about some talk show and concerns with the foundation?"

Shawna opened her mouth and closed it again. "I didn't. Layla mentioned something though. Said the foundation was already getting bad press. And, of course, it was connected to sports." Layla not only worked at Cornerstone, she was also a survivor of domestic abuse.

"Hmm. I wish we knew what was said exactly and how that fit with our 'emergency' meeting."

Dr. Hanreddy chortled. "Me? I think it's odd that it was such an emergency, yet the meeting still hasn't been rescheduled, not to mention since when is giving out money an emergency. These women here? They're the emergency."

No argument there. After more small talk, I visited and counseled as best I could with the residents at Cornerstone, cringing inside when I saw the two young girls. I couldn't imagine what they'd been through.

CHAPTER 9

The rest of the day was more relaxing. I took Jasper for a run in the park in the afternoon and we met up with Ronnie, Andy, and Elle. It was a beautiful day, sun shining and not too hot or too cold. Jasper was good with Elle and tolerated her less than gentle pets. They made such a happy family and at six months, Elle's bright personality was starting to come through.

I enjoyed the time with them and the friendship, yet I was a little jealous at the same time. Not only did Ronnie seem to have the perfect life with no frills, but she'd already lost all her pregnancy weight and regained her figure. She still glowed and her red hair never seemed to need taming. Not to mention, she and Andy were so obviously in love.

Shaking off the melancholy, I decided a stop at the Yoga Pod was in order, and maybe a good run without Jasper. I shuddered to think maybe I should eat less Rocky Road ice cream.

Showered and energized, I flipped on the news. Timing is everything and I caught "…hopefully, someone from the Noth Foundation can clear this up" right before the cut to a commercial. I watched the rest of the news, however the topic wasn't revisited. My phone buzzed. CallerID told me it was Ted's father, Hamilton Noth, and I ignored the call.

I called Jillian instead. "Hey. How're you doing? Did you happen to catch anything on the news about the foundation?"

"I didn't. Wade mentioned something, so let me put him on."

"Hi, Stacie. Not sure what I can tell you. That talk show last night, well, Barbie Blake apparently accused Kevin McNair of paying off someone so he could be on the foundation board for some nefarious purpose. He, of course, denied the act and the motivation. Blake then went on a rampage attacking him and athletes in general. Although she never offered what she believed to be the nefarious purpose, she implied the foundation was going to whitewash any domestic violence by athletes."

"But wait! No one by that name is on the Board. The representative from the Sports Commission is Austin Beasley, not Kevin McNair. And why would this Barbie person want to malign the Foundation?"

"Sorry, I can't help you there."

"Wade, what do you know about Beasley and McNair?"

"Beasley is older. He retired from the NFL a few years ago. He'd played football – defensive end – for most of his career, tried his hand at broadcasting when he got injured, and seems to have a knack for the public relations stuff. He's a big dude for sure, but calm and…"

"Cuddly. He's cuddly." Jillian piped in and Wade laughed.

"Okay, cuddly. He can easily work a crowd instead of plowing through one. He moved to the PR stuff and it's a good fit. If Blake said Beasley's job was to paint a glowing picture of sports, I'd almost get that. He wouldn't lie and he wouldn't ignore facts, but his demeanor would be so positive, the information would not necessarily have the same punch. He could probably tell someone they had a terminal illness and they'd thank him. His motivation? Plain and simple. He loves the game."

"Okay, so what about McNair?"

"McNair plays or played basketball – maybe some football early on. For lots of athletes, sport is a job or a skill that can get you an education or at least move you up the social ladder. For McNair, basketball was his ticket. He plays in the NBA but isn't a star. He's never been one of those athletes who ended up in the news. I like his style on the court and I'm not sure… I didn't realize he wasn't still playing."

"Weird. I have a listing of who's on the board and he's not listed. Oh, well. I guess Langford will fill us in eventually."

"The negative stuff in the media is spreading like wildfire with less facts than emotion, and your name is associated with it thanks to Blake. You using that alarm system?"

I hedged the answer. One day removed, and I was out of the habit. "Message received."

Wade gave the phone back to Jillian. My phone buzzed and I groaned. "Hamilton Noth left me a voice mail. What now?"

We disconnected and I played the voicemail message.

"Stacie, I can't imagine what you're doing that you couldn't take a phone call from me. You need to take care of business and keep my son's name and his foundation out of the news, you hear me?"

I shook my head and decided maybe I'd been too cavalier about the emails from Langford and his staffers over the past few months. I checked the last email with foundation business and wrote down all the emails. I tried to remember who each person was and what I knew about them.

The women were easy. Aside from Shawna, Dr. Hanreddy, and me, Alexa Morales represented Reston Human Resources, and then there was Senator Clarisse Bryce whose major interests were revitalization, women's rights, and racial issues. At least that's what her website indicated.

This last email I received from Langford didn't include Beasley nor did it include McNair, yet it included the right number of people. Odd. Sometimes, the emails included Smythe, sometimes not. Sometimes they included the Police Chief, Rizzo, other times the Fire Chief, Petkra, sometimes both. I wondered how many I wasn't on.

A quick search and I had all the emails I received related to the foundation and not a one mentioned either of the professional athletes. Beasley's email appeared on some of them though. Instead of using a group name,

Langford must have included whoever he remembered at the moment.

I meticulously documented how addressees changed when another email came in. Langford had rescheduled our meeting to Monday with assurances that there would be security in the parking garage. I checked the recipients and added to my list. My head hurt and after a quick dinner from the freezer and a glass of wine, I talked Jasper into watching a movie on Netflix. *Oceans 8* was just the thing.

CHAPTER 10

Nate, my father, Ted's attorney Cyrus Trichter, and Hamilton Noth made sure I knew rumors were spreading about the foundation and potential funny business over the rest of the weekend and all day Monday. Obviously, my mind didn't work that way – I still couldn't figure out how a nonprofit foundation, barely incorporated, could get this much bad press. It was all very vague with nothing to latch onto. Hopefully, the meeting would clear up the confusion. Perhaps, Lionel Smythe would have some answers.

At the Langford Building, I spotted two security guards before I parked and hesitated as I approached the elevator. Someone reached from behind me to hit the call button and I jumped.

"Sorry, I didn't mean to startle you." It was him, the same man who'd plowed into me with the piercing blue eyes. The apparent root of the funny business rumors.

He held the elevator door so it couldn't close. "Are you going up?" I stared at him and his smile disappeared, his expression softening. "I'll get one of the security guards if it will make you feel safer."

"No, no. That's okay. Just surprised. I didn't hear you come up behind me." I stepped into the elevator and he followed. As the door was about to close, I said, "Wait! There's Shawna."

Shawna hustled and we rode up in the elevator. As we exited on the twelfth floor, he turned to us. "I'm Kevin McNair by the way. And you are?"

"Stacie Maroni. And this is Shawna Jackson."

Shawna extended her hand and he shook it. "Nice to meet you both." He looked down the hall and then added, "Do you happen to know where this meeting is?"

"The email said the conference room."

He waved us forward and pretty soon we could hear people talking and zeroed in on the noise. The conference room was large with a full bar at one end. Shawna's raised brows registered the same surprise I felt. Leaving McNair to his own devices, we drifted over to Alexa Morales, Sarah Hanreddy, and Senator Bryce. The five women on the board, ostensibly balanced by five men.

The order of the day was small talk and I took advantage of the opportunity to look around the room and watch the others. I noticed the wall of pictures. Langford getting an award. Langford giving someone a check. Langford with his wife on his arm at what looked like a casino night. There was another one of Langford with his daughter, Meredith, and one of Langford and his wife at Colonial Downs. I recognized the dining room of the country club in another.

The bar was conveniently positioned at the end of the same wall. I shifted my focus to the growing number of people in the room. An interesting, if not motley crowd, from the slim, long-haired smiling bartender I guessed to be in his fifties to the portly glad-handing Senator probably not much older, but clearly not having much fun no matter how much he smiled.

Shawna must have caught my puzzled expression as she leaned in and asked, "What's wrong?"

My gaze swept the room again. I whispered, "Too many people here. It's like the board exploded like rabbits. Why invite people to a board meeting who aren't on the board?"

Shawna's jaw tensed and she looked around the room, a slight head nod as she counted. "Sixteen, ten men, plus Langford. Should be fourteen max, even counting the bartender. I sure hope someone feeds that man."

At that point, Langford rang a bell and I groaned. "Could everyone please take a seat so we can begin. We're still waiting on one person, but he's on his way." He paused to let everyone move toward the table before he continued.

"First, I'd like to introduce Jacob Hardy. He's a business major at George Mason and has agreed to serve as our Administrative Assistant. He'll be responsible for keeping minutes, correspondence, and generally ensuring that the Theodore Noth Foundation lives up to the expectations set forth in our Articles of Incorporation and Bylaws. Please welcome Jacob."

Everyone clapped and Jacob looked up briefly from his computer and immediately put his head back down. His hand shook and he kept making furtive glances around the room as Langford continued.

"To my left is Lionel Smythe, Esquire. Lionel will be handling legal issues specific to the Foundation and its nonprofit status. I think he has spoken to everyone. Please welcome Mr. Smythe."

The short slim man with a crewcut and bowtie nodded in response to the applause. He so looked like I'd imagined him, I almost cheered.

Langford continued to talk, mostly highlighting Ted's wishes and spouting platitudes about the difference the foundation could make for not only the victims of domestic violence, but in preventing domestic violence through mental health. He paused strategically as is typical for politicians and pastors and got head nods and smiles.

While he preached, I pulled out my briefcase and the list of names from that stack of emails. I started checking off who was present I could recognize, only I ran out of names before I ran out of people, and one thing was for sure. Austin Beasley was not present.

Langford took a breath and a sip of his drink and Smythe spoke up. "Senator Langford, for my sake at least, and probably Jacob's as well, could everyone please introduce themselves and their function with the Board?"

At a loss for words and not used to being upstaged, Langford stumbled a bit. "I guess we could do that. Umm. Ladies, first. Mrs. Noth, why don't you start?"

"I'll start with a correction on my name. Stacie Maroni for the records, Jacob, Mr. Smythe. Senator Langford asked me to serve on the Board as Theodore Noth was my husband and I worked with Ted on many activities related to domestic violence. I also volunteer as a trauma counselor."

Each of us women then introduced ourselves. As the men were about to start, another man who fit my stereotypic image of a football player lumbered into the room. He waved off Langford and took a seat behind Shawna and me. I noticed Shawna's wide-eyed expression and smiled.

Matching up who said what with the lists and correspondence to date was a challenge. The late comer, as I guessed, was none other than Austin Beasley. Everyone introduced, Langford tried to continue his planned speech but to no avail.

"Wait a minute Senator. I have the Articles of Incorporation and Conflict of Interest Statements and something's wrong here." Smythe shook his head. "For starters, where's Tyler Kearns? He's listed on the filing papers and I have a COI for him."

Langford looked around the room and then to Jacob. "Jacob?"

"Yes, sir?" His fingers flew and then he looked up. "I have a record here for a Dr. Tyler Kearns, psychologist, appointed to the Board on August 1st by agreement of Senator William Langford, J. Colton Stewart, and Fire Chief Bruce Petkra."

"Well, then why isn't he here?"

I could tell from Jacob's fingers flying and head moving he was searching and then he stopped. He looked up and very quietly stated, "You didn't include him in the announcement of the meeting, sir."

Smythe put his head in his hands and I choked back a laugh, while Langford stumbled. "Must have missed him. We'll catch him up. No big deal. Getting back…"

Smythe cleared his throat. "Senator, a few more questions first. Of the five male members of the Board, he's the only one missing, yet there are seven males who just introduced themselves as members of the board. Some are listed on the papers that were filed. Some I have the COI for." He paused. "Mr. McNair, I have neither record of you. So, I have to ask, how did you end up here?"

"Excuse me? I called to ask about the foundation and talked to the senator. We met for lunch and he invited me to the meeting. Then I received this letter from him." He retrieved an envelope from his inside jacket pocket and handed it to Mr. Smythe.

Mr. Smythe put his hand up to stop Langford from speaking and directed his comment to Jacob. "Any record there, son?" As he waited, he opened the letter.

Jacob was apparently anticipating this. He cleared his throat. "Yes, sir. Mr. Kevin McNair, appointed to the Board on August 15st by agreement of Senator Langford, J. Colton Stewart, and Chief Petkra."

"Yet his name is not on the Articles of Incorporation. In fact, depending on the paperwork I reviewed from the Board, the names of the male members of the Board seem to shimmer and change. I suspect it was these inconsistencies that Ned Anderson, may he rest in peace, discovered and was concerned about."

"I'm sure that will be easily cleared up, right Jacob?" Senator Langford smiled and waited. As did we all. Jacob looked to Smythe.

"Senator, the board can't meet until it is cleared up. Everyone here believes they are on the board. That can't be and the incorporation and nonprofit status cannot move forward. In fact, nothing can move forward."

Lots of shifting in seats occurred. Finally, Beasley asked, "Mr. Smythe, I think we get your point. We can't make decisions because we don't know who the decision-makers are for this foundation. Soon after Mr. Noth's passing some of us met. At Mr. Noth's bequest, Senator Langford was designated to direct the foundation. Those of us present agreed on two things initially – there would be ten members of the Board, equally representing males and females, consistent with what we were told were Noth's wishes. Decisions for who was on the Board would be made by no less than two already confirmed members and Senator Langford."

There were a few nods around the table and Chief Rizzo leaned back. That was a meeting I was not invited to and I wondered who else had or had not been there. On the other hand, I was pleasantly surprised they had at least articulated a process. The question remained, though, who confirmed anyone after Langford.

Beasley continued, "Jacob, is there any record of that meeting and those decisions?"

Jacob searched and shook his head. Smythe grimaced.

"Senator Langford. As legal counsel, I suggest we adjourn this meeting. Based on the paperwork I received from Mr. Trichter, the codicil for the Foundation specifically stipulates you as Director, and Ms. Maroni and Mr. Stewart as designated members of the Board. The remaining eight were to represent specific stakeholders."

He paused as everyone digested that information. "Jacob and I will determine what we can and propose next steps. Mr. Stewart and Chief Petkra? As you were mentioned with regard to both of the men I queried about, please forward any emails or correspondence specific to the Foundation to Jacob at your earliest convenience."

Langford deflated, battle lost. "Anything else, anyone?"

Senator Bryce stood. "Obviously, the female members are not the issue. I do question if any of us were even considered to participate in the vetting of the male board members. In particular, given concerns raised publically by a talk show host, having some indication of the vetting process would seem appropriate if it is to be above reproach."

I wasn't the only one who turned to McNair. His color rose and he didn't respond for a few seconds. He looked around the room. "I have no ulterior motive in my interest in serving on the Board, or at least none nefarious. I have a family member who was the victim of domestic violence. I know what effects it can have on a child and a family."

Simply stated. Nothing but self-control and no blame.

Smythe handed the senator a piece of paper. Langford looked up long enough to say "Meeting adjourned. The bar is still open if you're inclined."

CHAPTER 11

That was enough for me. Shawna, Smythe and I made it to the elevator ahead of the crowd. In the parking garage, we were parting ways when Smythe called my name.

"What do you think happened, Ms. Maroni-not-Noth?" The twinkle in his eye conveyed his approval of my correcting the senator.

"Best guess? Nobody was tracking who was asked or who was on the Board. The papers were initiated by Mr. Trichter as Executor of Ted's will and he received ten names from someone, did his thing and sent it over to the admin and you to deal with. Only with no one keeping records... I know I was never sent the incorporation paperwork or bylaws to look at. I wasn't at the meeting Beasley referred to either. I'm not sure..."

A shot rang out and shattered the window of the car next to us. I grabbed onto Smythe and dropped to the ground, pulling him with me. More shots fired, lots of shouting, and then silence.

"All clear. This is Chief Rizzo and all's clear."

Smythe looked at me as if to ask, "Do you believe him?"

I shrugged and stood up long enough to yell "Over here!" and dropped to the ground again. At least my jeans protected my knees from scrapes and the dirt and residue. Within seconds, we were looking up at Chief Rizzo and McNair. I registered McNair slipping what looked like a gun inside his jacket and Rizzo's gun in his hand at his side.

McNair extended his hands and pulled me up – a déjà vu moment – as Rizzo did the same with Smythe.

"What happened? We heard shots as we came out of the elevator."

"Someone shot at us." Smythe stated the obvious as he pointed at the shattered front window of his car.

As if it explained the shots, I added, "We were standing here talking."

"Mr. Smythe is that your car?" Smythe nodded as he looked at the damage to his Prius.

"Officers are on the way. They'll take your report. Unless the bullet can be found easily, we'll impound your car."

"Chief Rizzo, what happened to the security guards? Where'd they go?"

"Guards, Stacie? As in more than one? We found one. He'd been knocked out cold."

"I saw two when I pulled into the garage. One closer to the elevator and one farther back."

McNair nodded. "I was right behind her and saw both of them. One more visible, one more furtive, hiding."

Officer McDonald and another officer pulled up next to us. They took our information and then it got crazy.

"Chief, dispatch just advised media have picked up the incident and are approaching the garage."

I don't know who looked more like a deer in the headlights, McNair or me. I looked at the Chief and he said, "Get away from here. Now."

I bolted for my car and was about to hop in and McNair stopped me. "My car is right there. Tinted windows. No connection to you."

I was weighing the options and heard one of the newscasters. Hide by myself or with McNair? He opened his passenger door and mouthed "your choice" as he ducked and walked around the car. There were only a few cars still in the garage and no way I'd be able to leave. I got in and closed the door. This way, if they realized it was my car over there, they'd presume I was still upstairs.

"Here's my plan. As the rest of the party breaks up, comes down, and gets in their cars and drives out, we can just follow them out. Hopefully, with all the confusion, they won't be sure who came out when, even if Langford is dumb enough to give them the whole guest list."

I nodded. "Sounds like a good plan. Who was still up there?"

"The two senators were having a shouting match and Beasley was trying to referee. He's actually pretty good at that. The Stewart guy and the Fire Chief were huddled together. My guess? It looks like they stepped in it and they're trying to get their stories straight. Jacob looked scared to death and the bartender was enjoying the show. Did anybody happen to think about confidentiality agreements? Insider news on conflicts among foundation members. Duck down, someone's coming."

I did as I was told. "Senator Bryce. Hmm. She actually drove herself. Nice Mercedes."

"Why did you tell me to duck?"

He laughed. "Instinct. The last time I was parked with a beautiful woman, I didn't want to get caught and no one would have believed the situation was innocent. I'm not sure they would now either."

He chuckled again and his blue eyes twinkled. "There goes Petkra. Your turn and I'll follow you out of the garage. Do you need me to follow you home?"

"No. No, I'll be fine. I'm sure whoever it was is long gone what with media and police all over the place. Thanks."

I quickly moved from his car to mine and followed the other cars out. One of the newscasters made eye contact as I tried to figure out what was going on. I shrugged and acted like any other person passing an accident or police situation, curious. McNair wasn't far behind me and he also slowed at the scene, rubbernecking with the best of them.

The drive home was uneventful. McNair turned off a block from the parking garage. I intentionally drove in circles and grabbed a coffee from the drive-through at a fast food chain. Awful coffee, but it gave me a chance to think and hopefully thwart anyone who might be following me, including McNair. I felt safer back in Beckman Springs with friends in the police department.

That night, I didn't need a reminder to arm the security system.

CHAPTER 12

Instead of the alarm or Jasper, I was awakened by the persistent ringing of my doorbell. It was only 6 a.m. As I lumbered down the stairs, Jasper scampered at my feet and my uninvited caller leaned on the doorbell again.

"I'm coming. I'm coming." My brain kicked in on the way to the door and I flipped open my laptop and pulled up the security view. Rick and Flatt were the culprits robbing me of my sleep. Judging from the uniforms, this was not a social call. I disarmed the security system and opened the door. As Rick opened his mouth, I pointed to the camera.

"What's the problem?" I shifted my gaze from one to the other and stepped back, inviting them to come in. Jasper immediately went to Rick – they had a mutual admiration thing going on. The picture of the small Maltese and the tall hunky cop always made me smile.

"I need coffee."

In the kitchen, I let Jasper out and fixed myself a cup.

"You going to tell me why you woke me up?"

Rick deferred to Flatt, obviously not a morning person. He read from his note pad. "Someone called in a complaint of a suspicious person in the neighborhood, man, heavy set, dressed in dark clothes, looking in your windows."

My mouth dropped.

"Stacie, did you have the alarm set by any chance? You or Jasper hear anything?"

Rick knew once things settled down I'd stopped using the alarm and had turned off all the notifications from the cameras of every time a bird flew by a camera. He'd nagged me about it every time he came over.

"Yes, the alarm was set and cameras running. Notifications were off though." I pulled up the app and turned the screen so he and Flatt could check the video feeds while I got caffeinated.

"There." Rick flipped it back to me. "Not much light though. Do you recognize the person?"

The image was dark on dark. Whoever it was, the hoodie covered their hair and shielded most of their face. I glanced at the kitchen window and then at Rick. "Probably your height, heavier or maybe just looks that way because of the sweats. This could be anybody."

I shook my head.

Flatt watched the video feed a few more seconds. "Nice system here. You check the feed often?"

"No." I shrugged. "Haven't had a reason to, no suspicious activity. At least not here."

"Anything else we should know about?" They both stood ready to leave. Rick shuffled on his feet.

I hesitated and Rick stared at the ceiling, his typical behavior when he was trying not to say something.

"Last week someone slashed a tire on my car when I was at yoga, and then someone tried to put a tracking device on my car at work. Makes no sense to me."

Flatt's eyes widened. Rick's smug expression told me he already knew about both those incidents. Marina Napoli most likely told him.

"Anything else?"

"I'm sure it has nothing to do with this. There've been some problems with Ted's foundation the last couple of weeks." I shrugged. "That was in Reston, though, not here in Beckman Springs."

Flatt scribbled something down. "We checked the perimeter. No sign of damage or attempted break in. Use your fancy security system here and call if you see anything suspicious. Got it?"

I nodded and they left. I watched Rick walk around my car, checking with a flashlight. He finished and as if he knew I was watching, gave me a "thumbs up." I fed Jasper and much too late I looked in the mirror. Good thing I wasn't still interested in Rick – hair a mess, no makeup, and my cotton jammies had seen better days. On the other hand, at least I wasn't wearing my one negligee. Maybe I needed to invest in a bathrobe.

I ran upstairs to get dressed for work. News of the shooting traveled fast and my father called before I made it out the door.

"Nate just called and I watched the news clip. Are you okay? Maybe you should make up with that cop."

"I'm fine. No one was hurt. The Reston police are investigating. I'm sure they will take care of security in the future."

Conveniently not telling him the cops had just been there, or that there'd been two security guards, I did my best to reassure him. I cuddled with Jasper until he disconnected after delivering a lecture on staying safe.

At work, Jillian waited at my office with my favorite Dunkin' Donuts coffee and muffin. She glanced down the hall, then tilted her head toward my office. Inside, she glared.

"You were on the news again, Stacie. Reinhardt is not going to be happy. Neither is your dad. You and the Noth Foundation. A shooter in the parking garage? What's going on?"

"I don't know. Smythe, the legal counsel, and I were talking by his car. Someone shot at us, or at least at his car. No one was hurt, except one of the security guards Langford had posted there."

There was a knock on my door sounding the arrival of Rosie, Trina, and Ronnie. Trina at least had the foresight to come armed with more coffee and donuts. We talked about the shooting.

The rest of the day went by without any crises. Kayla Anderson stopped by to thank me for my help. The police still didn't have any leads and as far as she knew, still considered it a random mugging. I wasn't so sure. And I was beginning to hope that, like a cat, I had nine lives.

CHAPTER 13

Lionel Smythe called and invited me to lunch at the Fried Tomato. Not particularly a health food aficionado, I'd never eaten there. On the other hand, it was a short walk from Foster's and the crisp edge of the fall breeze felt good.

As I walked in my mouth dropped. Lionel sat in a red booth that reminded me of a very ripe tomato complete with a green leaf on each side. There were several of these. I spotted some larger, more elongated booths that were eggplant purple. Our table looked like a slice of zucchini. I saw another that looked like a slice of onion. All the décor was vegetable themed. Different to say the least and I had trouble focusing on Lionel with all the veggie distractions.

"Hi. Sorry, I've never been inside before. This is …"

He grinned. "Unique. The food's good, it's quiet, and inside our little tomato here, we should have a bit of privacy."

We discussed the menu and placed our orders. I had lots of questions bubbling in my head, but I waited for him to start.

He sipped on his tea and exhaled. "Last night. In my area of law, being shot at isn't the expectation. You okay?"

"Yeah. At least this time, I wasn't hit." His mouth dropped and I smiled. "Long story, another time. How about you?"

"I'm trying to wrap my head around the foundation and why someone is attacking it." He shook his head. "By the way, the second security guard you saw? He wasn't really a security guard. Langford only hired one, the one who was knocked out."

My mouth dropped. That must have been why Chief Rizzo thought there was only one.

"Wow. How is he? Wait, how did someone know to dress up just like the one that was hired?"

"The guard is doing okay. How did the fake guard know? I have no idea. Maybe the senator always uses the same company and the fake guard knew that. Didn't even have to know one had been hired. If he was the only one and looked official, no one would have questioned him being there."

"You're right. As for the foundation, I'm with you on that. It's not like the goal of the foundation or any of the activities the foundation might support are controversial. No harm to animals or children, no environmental issues, not even anything extreme left or right. Ted's intent was to educate and prevent domestic violence in all forms and provide appropriate care for victims. Maybe someone who was convicted of domestic violence? Feels domestic violence is part of the world order?" I didn't have an explanation.

He shook his head. "If not the mission of the foundation, then what? One man died and we've been shot at. Why?"

"Someone angry about who is on the board, how the members were selected? Technically, this is Langford's baby now. Someone trying to make him look bad? There have been no grants given out or projects even reviewed, so it's not retaliation for being treated unfairly. Did you and Jacob figure out the hows and whats of the extra board members?"

He laughed. "Jacob is very thorough, probably pathologically so, and catalogued every email of Langford's or his staffers that had the word 'foundation' in it. No easy chore as Langford is on more than one foundation. He's contacting everyone who was at the meeting or was ever mentioned on the emails and asking them to forward him any correspondence related to the foundation."

He shook his head and continued. "He discovered Langford used his staffers to handle correspondence – three different staffers, all working from the same initial list of possible people to fit the descriptors from Ted's legacy."

"Oh my. You're telling me they didn't talk to each other or Langford?"

"Not always. Sometimes. As I mentioned at the meeting, Trichter shared with me that along with setting up the foundation, Ted's will stipulated Langford, Stewart, and you. Now, given that, if he or I had been part of the process, the three of you would have been the ones vetting the rest of the Board."

"That would make sense, but that's not what happened, obviously."

"Nope. Staffers were given a list of people from Langford." With an eye roll, he added, "He can't recall where that list came from. He's sure Trichter gave him those names as suggestions from Ted or you may have." His eyebrows and voice raised at that.

"I suggested Shawna and Dr. Hanreddy. I also told him to contact other local support groups for survivors."

"So, there's this list of people with the assumption that not everyone will agree to do this as it is volunteer. There has to be some payback or motivation. For the sports industry, good will with the public. For the two senators, good will with their constituents. Others, the motivation is likely more personal."

I nodded. That would be the obvious explanation for Ted specifically naming Stewart. "And somehow, Petkra must have agreed next? Please don't tell me he was the next male who agreed."

"Petkra is the next one who agreed or indicated interest. But he was technically not vetted, other than by virtue of his position as Fire Chief. Following that logic, Chief Rizzo should have been an automatic confirm as well. By then though, Langford decided to add in the review by three existing members, but included himself. Only there's no record of that meeting with Beasley and the others. At the same time, after that Beasley was not invited or included in other emails. The vetting committee ended up a good ol' boy group."

"Hold it. What prompted him to do that? Was anyone refused board membership?"

"Therein lies the other problem. No one was refused membership on the board. One person – Kevin McNair – contacted Langford to ask about the board, and in his usual manner, Langford courted, glad-handed, and added him. And nobody told the staffers to stop contacting people on the list when the board seats were filled."

"I'm afraid to ask. How many people think they are on the Board as a result?"

"At least fifteen with twice as many males as females." He leaned back.

"Ouch. How's Langford fixing this mess?"

Lionel shook his head. "He's working to figure out a solution or so he says. Sorry. Both Trichter and I strongly suggested that you and Stewart review the others to fill the remaining eight seats with alternates if appropriate. And set term limits and the process for filling vacancies. We also supported Senator Bryce's request that women need to be involved at every decision point. No more decision-making by a solely male committee. I'm sending you the information – dossiers on all of them. Also to Stewart. Technically, Langford only has a vote if the two of you disagree."

"Anything else you found?"

He glanced around the room as he leaned forward again. He cleared his throat. "The other issue Ned Anderson likely discovered? Apparently, there was a grant awarded by the foundation. It's in the correspondence and Jacob is trying to find the paper trail."

"What? That's not possible. The Board hasn't even established the application process or anything."

Lionel signaled with his hand for me to lower my voice. "No money has changed hands. Until the incorporation papers are signed, there is no foundation, and by default, no access to the funds. We told Langford he needs to notify the grantee there was a miscommunication."

"Oh, and somehow there was a deposit made to the foundation account. I have a call in to Trichter, and Jacob is using his technology skills to try to chase that down as well."

I exhaled and leaned back. I had a lot more questions now. Both our phones buzzed at the same time. With hasty goodbyes, Lionel picked up the check. "Expense account – business lunch." He winked as he plodded off.

CHAPTER 14

The tension in my muscles from the day and night before didn't get any better and I needed some relief. I dashed home, took care of Jasper, and then drove back to the Yoga Pod. I managed to find a parking spot directly under a light and closer than where I'd parked last week. As I walked into the studio, I froze. Kevin was warming up and chatting with the instructor.

I turned away from him, smiled to the closest group of women, started my stretches, and tried to find my focus. Not for long, not successfully.

The women were chatting and I listened in as the curvy blonde commented, "I'm so glad the legislature finally agreed to make gambling legal. I mean, I drive to the casinos in Maryland, but it will be so much fun to have one closer, hopefully with a spa and great restaurants."

"I always lose, even at the charity casino nights. A few weeks ago, I attended one at the country club for breast cancer research. It was fun and all you could lose was your donation to walk in the door, but some man got very upset." Josie, the quiet one shrugged.

I tried to imagine a casino night at the country club and I was glad of the instructor's call to get started. As the class ended, Kevin came over to me. "Can I buy you a cup of coffee?"

I nodded. I had a lot of questions for him, starting with how he just happened to be there at the same time I was. I followed him and we walked to the Starbucks.

"What will you have?"

"Skinny Mocha, please." I reached into my bag and he waved his hand at me.

"My treat. Table?"

I nodded and gravitated to one in the far corner as a couple vacated. Comfy arm chairs and big enough to require space around them. Not that I was feeling vulnerable or anything, I watched as the barista handed him the two cups and he walked over. Tall, athletic yet slim, he walked as if stiff, no sway to his body.

"Here we go. Two Skinny Mochas." He pulled napkins out of his pocket and added them to the table. I heard a slight wince as he sat down.

"Are you hurt?"

He shrugged it off. "Sport has a way of beating up the body. My physical therapist recommended yoga last year for the stretch and the control. How long have you been doing yoga?"

"About a year. Is this your first time at Yoga Pod? I don't remember seeing you here before."

"Another thing about sport, you have a home base, but you travel a lot. Especially during the season. So, for the past year, I have collected locations for highly recommended yoga studios from other players, physical therapists along the way, and, when all else fails, the internet. One day, ATs – athletic trainers – may get on board."

I fiddled with my coffee, still waiting for the explanation of how he ended up at my yoga studio. He must have sensed something was off.

"I'm sorry. Did I say something wrong?"

"You didn't answer my question. About Yoga Pod."

His brows furrowed and he looked confused. Pulling out his phone, he went to some app and showed me a map. "A friend created this app for me. It searches all the yoga studios and their ratings and shows me where they are. Then I can enter my rating in after I go so the next circuit around I know if I want to go back there or find some place new."

He pointed to Yoga Pod. It showed that he had been there three times before tonight and rated it either a 4 or 5. The first time had been a month ago. I relaxed a little, though obviously he could have entered that data any time.

"Okay. You ran into me as I was leaving Yoga Pod last week. You were in a hurry. Do you remember that?"

He smiled and shook his head. "I remember knocking someone down, yes. I hadn't made the connection though. Sorry. I was running late and needed to catch a train. But I hadn't been at the studio that day. Another appointment in another building."

I nodded and drank my coffee.

"Stacie, you seem suspicious and after being shot at the other night, I don't blame you. Nobody shot at me, yet I seem to have become fodder for the talk show hosts and even sports commentators. My agent isn't exactly thrilled, but that's another story. You have the inside track on this foundation. What is going on?"

I shrugged. "Unfortunately, my only first-hand knowledge is what was stipulated in legalese with Ted's life insurance policy and the codicil – the mission, the general configuration of the board, and the funds with stipulations that some proportion be invested initially so that interest could keep the foundation going in perpetuity."

Head shaking, he didn't say anything for a few minutes. "Weird."

"For sure. It makes no sense to me." My phone buzzed and it was Rick. Rude probably, but I took the call as he had stopped calling me for personal reasons over a month ago.

"Stacie, you need to get home. Someone just tried to break in – same neighbor called it in. Where are you?"

"Starbucks by the Yoga Pod. I'll be there in 10 minutes." I stood as I was talking and Kevin followed suit. "I'm sorry. That was the police. They're at my house. I gotta go."

I grabbed my bag and bolted from Starbucks. Kevin was right behind and then beside me. At my car, he stopped me before I hopped in. He dropped down and used his phone as a flashlight.

"What are you doing?"

"I may be a media target, but it's beginning to look a lot more personal for you. Checking for anything that doesn't belong."

"And you know how to do that because?"

He stood up and deadpanned, "Please Stacie, I'm more than just a pretty face and athletic prowess."

He laughed at my expression. "I worked security for a while in college before I got on a college team and then off seasons to help my family out financially before I went pro. I'm thinking you should be okay. It's too well-lit here for anyone to have tampered too badly without being seen. And if they'd managed to get inside without your fob, I think the alarm would go off. He handed me a business card. Humor me? Text me when you get home so I know you're safe."

I took the card and drove home.

CHAPTER 15

Rick and O'Hare greeted me as I stepped out of my car, gym bag over my shoulder. I could hear Jasper barking in the background. Another officer walked toward us.

"The alarm company notified us about the same time as your neighbor. Whoever it was managed to breech a contact on the kitchen door, setting off the alarm. Probably the same person as before. You must have your notifications turned off. We need to see your video feed."

O'Hare was all business and even though he's not much older than me, his tone was patronizing. I half expected him to give me a gold star for having the alarm on. I entered the house and looked at the alarm. It said "RESET" and I had no clue what that meant. While they looked at video, I called Reston Security.

Reston Security verified the police were on site, my identity, and reset the system. They'd have someone swing by the next day to check the kitchen door, but it looked good from their end. O'Hare watched the video and Rick got Jasper calmed down, then went back outside.

"Stacie. I need you to save this set of clips here and send them to me."

I stopped pacing and sat down, spinning the laptop toward me. Wade had shown me how to do this and I pulled up the notes tab, and ignoring O'Hare's wide-eyed look of surprise, I followed the directions to download the marked clips. I'm no dummy.

"Email address?" I moved the laptop so O'Hare could type it in himself.

"We'll get this on the news and see if anyone can recognize the person. There are a couple of clips here you need to look at."

Rick walked in and cleared his throat. "I think we're through here. Anything else you need from us?"

"Nope. You're all set. We did get some footage so I'll finish up here."

Rick left and O'Hare found the other clips he wanted me to look at. Cars on the street. "Any look out of place?"

"Geesh. I don't know. My neighbors have guests all the time. I don't keep track."

O'Hare snickered. "Actually, the camera that includes the end of the driveway? You have footage of every car that's gone past your driveway."

I groaned. "I don't think I want to tell my neighbors that." Talk about violation of privacy.

He left and with Jasper in my lap, I texted Kevin to let him know I was home. Then I called Jillian and Wade. I must have sounded stressed out and they drove over.

Wade re-checked everything on the security system, the kitchen door, and ran some tests. I mentioned the incident with the tracker and he ran out the door before I could stop him. He proudly proclaimed, "Nothing there. You're good" as he came back in.

I laughed. "Glad to hear it. You're the third person to check it so I'm glad the first two didn't miss anything."

He scowled. "Who were the other two?"

I sat up, surprised at his reaction. "Kevin, when I was parked at Yoga Pod tonight, and before that, Rick, here last night."

"Kevin?"

"McNair. We were at Starbucks when Rick called about the alarm going off."

"And you asked him to check for a tracker?"

"No. He stopped me before I got in the car. Checked the outside to see if he could spot anything that didn't belong. I asked him about it and he said he worked security before going pro."

Wade nodded, but the set of his jaw told me he wasn't convinced by the explanation.

"Jillian can pick you up for work tomorrow. The parking lot is too large and no security. It would be too easy for someone to tamper with your car. After tonight, I think you have to accept the fact that someone's after you, not just Ted's foundation."

"But who? It doesn't make sense to me."

Jillian patted my arm. "Let's think about this. Who might have a vendetta against Ted, the foundation, or you?"

I shook my head. "All the suspects from Ted's murder? Someone whose wife or girlfriend was at Cornerstone some time? I don't know. Smythe asked about Langford. Maybe it was someone with a grudge against him?"

"And you as a target will get back at him how?"

"Well, it might make the foundation and his leadership of it look bad." I tilted my head. "You know, we don't know that anyone else isn't having similar issues. Langford, Stewart, and I were identified in an email from Ned Anderson and mentioned on the news. It was Smythe's car that got shot up. But, yeah, this feels personal."

It was getting late and we all had to work in the morning. At Wade's insistence, I turned notifications back on so I was immediately being prompted of any sound or movement detected by any of the cameras. Not comforting. Wade suggested, for my peace of mind, I push the kitchen island against the door when I went to bed. Alarm set, cameras going, and the door blocked, sleep still didn't come easy.

CHAPTER 16

I was glad I could close my office door the next day as I kept yawning and my mind wandered at will. It probably wouldn't make any sense to the average person, but the tedious part of my work helped to keep me centered. Avoiding my friends and planning to use flex-time to leave early, I worked through lunch.

A beep alerted me to a text from the Senator. Curious as to what and why, I opened the message and groaned. The message simply stated "Given the circumstances last night, I would understand if you've reconsidered your association with the foundation." I could add him to the list of people suggesting just that.

A few minutes later, I received an email from him. The email explained what Smythe had already told me, but omitted any hint of responsibility by the senator himself. The email then directed me to evaluate the individuals whose files were attached and rank order males and females. It occurred to me the Senator used a lot of text and phone calls, as well as emails – Jacob probably would never have all the communications on the foundation.

Without hesitation, I opened the file labeled McNair. Wow. The picture provided was him on the basketball court, obviously during a practice as he was shirtless. And wow. The dossier someone had put together was short. Kevin Michael McNair was 38 years old, the oldest of five children from a small town outside of Baltimore. He'd played football and basketball in high school, then basketball for two different colleges. He was a free agent, whatever that meant, and was picked up. According to this, his contract was up at the end of the last season. He was divorced, no children.

The last part of the dossier included his request for information about the foundation due to his own experiences with domestic violence. Someone had made the notation of "sports industry" or "community at-large" for which seats he might fill. A numbers person at heart, I did the math – four years between high school and college were not accounted for in this dossier. This wasn't complete. I googled his name. Other than a lot more pictures of him on the court, nothing popped up, not even the now famous talk show interview.

Ready to escape early and read the rest of the dossiers, I remembered I had no wheels and had to wait for Jillian. I had plenty of work to do and managed to get ahead. As an afterthought to my defensive comment about not knowing if anyone else was being targeted, I called J. Colton Stewart and left a message. I didn't hear back from him and my only interruption was Reston Security. They'd meet me at my house at 6 o'clock to check the alarm system. Jillian drove me home and she and Wade came back later.

Security system dealt with, the three of us went to dinner at the local steakhouse. A glass of wine was definitely in order.

Taking a deep breath, I asked the question uppermost in my thoughts. "Wade, how much do you know about Kevin McNair? He keeps popping up, all too conveniently."

He high-fived me with a big smile. "Good job questioning motives and coincidences. I don't know too much. I did check around and he doesn't work part time for any of the security companies in the immediate area. His background check didn't reveal anything and that in itself was odd."

"Why was that odd?"

He shrugged. "My impression was that he came from working class, had been in trouble at some point as a youth, and sports turned him around. The 'trouble' part didn't exist in the background check – possibly sealed as a juvenile offender. Tell me what's bothering you."

Our dinners arrived and I filled them in between bites. "The night Smythe and I were shot at, I thought I saw… No, I'm sure. As he and Rizzo joined us, I'm pretty sure he had a gun. I know we're in the south and guns are common enough. Then he showed up at the Yoga place. And he checked my car, but he could have been planting something, though he obviously didn't. And the security thing seems like a flimsy explanation. Should I trust him?"

"I'm not sure I know the answer…yet. Be careful, Stacie."

"Stacie, are you interested in him?" Jillian asked with a big smile.

"I don't know. He seems nice enough. But there's something... He's almost too smooth and perfect. Besides, as a professional athlete, he must be rich and I'm done with rich. I'm a *Forever in Blue Jeans* girl."

They both laughed, yet I got the impression they didn't quite believe me.

Jillian drove me to work again and I realized just how much I valued my independence, not to mention my early morning yoga. This was only the second day and it was getting old fast. The morning passed by quickly with only one interruption – a phone call from J. Colton Stewart.

"Hi, Stacie. I got your message. What were you asking about?"

"Hi, Colton, thanks for calling me back. It seems like a lot of odd things – a slashed tire, for example – have been happening with me. I was wondering if you've experienced similar things."

"Yes and no. Right after our first meeting, someone broke into my office and trashed the place. The police and I guessed whoever it was probably wanted the latest game version, which of course was in the safe."

"Anything else?"

"Other than that, some guy cut me off, but, hey, I work in the city and drivers are crazy. My car and house alarms went off a few times. It was odd, the cameras on the house didn't pick up anything. The alarm company's explanation was that whoever it was managed to avoid the cameras."

He didn't sound concerned and I asked, "Are these all things that are common in your life? Or only since you've been associated with the foundation?"

He hesitated. "Huh. I never gave it much thought or connected the two. No one has threatened me or anything. Now that you ask it that way though, in any given year? Maybe the alarm company contacts me once. Maybe some idiot cuts me off. No one's ever broken into my office before, no reason to. There's no money kept there and all the game stuff is locked up every night or shredded. Probability for all these things to happen in this short amount of time? I could write a program and calculate it, but it's safe to say it's low. That's worrisome."

We chatted for a few minutes and then disconnected. I thought about what I knew now. Stewart also seemed to be a target. I'd emailed Shawna and gotten her response. She wasn't having any problems out of the ordinary. And she'd checked with Dr. Hanreddy, who also indicated everything was typical. Then again, their names weren't made public. It made me wonder if Langford was faring similarly.

CHAPTER 17

The week had already been taxing, then Langford topped it off by calling another meeting. At least this time, the meeting would not be at his building. One of the Hilton's small conference rooms would work fine and was more convenient. No elevators, valet parking, and if anyone wanted a drink, they had to go to the bar.

Jacob and Smythe were already in the room and plotting away when I arrived. "Here's the meeting agenda. Water for the senator. Presentation ready to go so everyone can see the documents."

Jacob nodded as Smythe punctuated each comment.

"Hi Jacob, Mr. Smythe. Sounds like you've got everything organized tonight."

They both nodded and Jacob's gaze moved to behind me. I couldn't read his expression and turned to see who triggered the half smile and clenched jaw.

Kevin and Stewart both entered the room. I still didn't have a feel for Stewart or his story and maybe it was none of my business. Actually, if I was honest with myself, his name alone – the pretentiousness of using a first initial as part of his name – didn't sit well. I tried to tell myself he didn't choose his name, someone else did, to no avail. Stewart had a cocktail and walked to the other end of the room. Kevin took the seat next to mine and I could feel the heat radiating from his body.

Everyone eventually arrived, some with drinks, most not. Langford had his bell with him though the absence of the bar made it less necessary for him to ring it.

"Good evening. I'm glad to see everyone here. We've been working hard to resolve some issues with board membership."

Several of the males groaned with furtive glances at the other males. Langford stopped talking and seemed reluctant to continue with the tension now apparent.

"Senator, perhaps I can explain?" Smythe interjected, breaking the silence. With Langford's nod, he commenced his explanation of the stipulations of the codicil to Ted's will. The slide presentation showed documents as he spoke.

"Given the codicil, the Chairperson and two members of the Executive Board were determined by Theodore Noth, unless they declined, of course. The remaining eight members should have been vetted by the initial two, with the Senator serving as the tie-breaker if needed. Clearly, that's not what happened. That is the process that Mr. Trichter, representing Mr. Noth and his estate, and I, on behalf of the foundation, recommended. I now have the results from both Ms. Maroni and Mr. Stewart."

Lots more grumbling and I tensed up from the scrutiny. Keeping my eyes on Smythe, I waited for him to continue.

"There were specific groups that needed to be represented. We have no conflicts on three of the remaining four women, representing survivor, medical care, and mental health/trauma services."

Senator Bryce stood up. "Please be seated Senator. There is no other woman in contention so you fill one of the community slots as the fifth woman." She sat back down appeased yet not happy.

He cleared his throat. "The other seat for which there is no contention is someone from the Sports Commission. Mr. Beasley is the person who officially represents the Commission. That leaves three additional slots to be filled – first responder and two community at-large slots. If we counted correctly, we have five who indicated interest. Chief Rizzo and Chief Petkra, our suggestion is that you both serve, however, alternate in terms of any decisions or alternate by years. Obviously, police, fire, and paramedics are critical first responders. We will leave it to the two of you to work that out."

The two men exchanged glances and nodded.

"That leaves Mr. Dimbody, Dr. Kearns, and Mr. McNair. All three were found to be acceptable by both Ms. Maroni and Mr. Stewart. Our suggestion is that we draw names – two of them. The third can serve as an alternate if either of the two selected is not able to serve. Is that agreeable gentlemen?"

The three nodded and Kevin leaned back. Jacob stood up and showed three index cards, one for each man. He dropped them in a bag and shook it. He then turned to Langford.

"Me? Why me?"

"That's your role. You reach in and pull out two cards." Smythe explained.

We all waited. Langford finally did the deed. He hesitated, paled, and then announced, "It's Kearns and McNair."

Smythe nodded. "Mr. Dimbody, thank you for your interest. You are more than welcome to stay for the rest of the meeting."

Mr. Dimbody smiled and leaned forward. I waited for him to speak, but he didn't say a word. He was a funny-looking man with his hair in tufts that were too short to cover his bald head and bushy eyebrows. So far, other than the obligatory introductions, he hadn't said a word. His dossier was short and only indicated he was interested and supported the mission.

Smythe then turned the meeting over to Langford and kept him to the agenda and the issues with the by-laws, terms of membership, and conflicts of interest. Very tedious and boring, and given the tension earlier, anticlimactic.

We were all about to fall asleep when the fire alarm sounded. Everyone moved out of the conference room and to the nearest exit. Kevin, Shawna, Smythe, Jacob, and I hung out together and watched as more and more people exited the hotel and fire trucks pulled up. I could see what looked like smoke on the other side of the hotel.

Chief Rizzo joined us after a few minutes. He continually scanned the area as he shared information. "Fire in the East wing. Someone set a cart on fire and then pushed it into a conference room. No one seriously injured. What's the likelihood, McNair?"

"I'm not a fan of coincidence, myself. The third meeting of this board and there's been an assault, shots fired, and now a fire. I think Dimbody lucked out."

Smythe nodded as did I.

I couldn't resist adding, "The other odd coincidence is random bad karma. A flat tire, someone tried to break into my house and into Stewart's office, getting cut off in traffic…"

The chief's jaw dropped. "You're not kidding, are you?" He looked at Shawna and she shook her head.

Jacob squeaked. We all looked at him. He opened his mouth and then shut it.

"Son, do you have something to tell us?" Smythe put his hand on the young man's shoulder.

"I do. Maybe. I'm not sure."

Chief Rizzo zeroed in on him. "Why don't you tell us and then we can decide if it is important or not."

Jacob nodded. "I have copies of all the correspondence on the foundation. From a search of all the emails of Langford and his staffers. I think you need to look at some of them. Then you can decide."

The chief stared off and then turned to Jacob. "Do you have those in your back pack there?"

Jacob nodded, his eyes wide.

"Smythe, you and Jacob, come with me. I think we need to look through all these emails and see what Jacob found. McNair, can you see to it these ladies get to their cars safely?"

"Yes, sir. I'll do that."

The three of them left and Shawna and I faced off against Kevin.

"You want to explain that? What did we miss?" I asked.

Kevin shrugged and grinned. "We bonded after the last meeting. No big deal."

I had the distinct impression there was more to it, but also recognized avoidance when I heard it. And maybe it was none of my business.

Shawna broke the silence. "Let's get out of here."

CHAPTER 18

My phone rang minutes after I walked in the door. CallerID alerted me it was McNair.

"Hello?"

"Kevin here, Stacie. I wanted to make sure you got home okay."

"Thanks. I did. And I have a pretty fancy alarm system and it is on." I wasn't sure why I added that other than that I was on edge.

"And to think I was going to ask if you at least had a ferocious dog or had self-defense training."

I laughed. "Jasper isn't usually ferocious, but he's warned me of unsavory and potentially dangerous people before – and he's been spot on." I smiled recalling his attack stance on two occasions previously. I didn't add my self-defense training. Some things might be better as a surprise.

"Maybe I need to meet Jasper and see if I pass the 'safe' test. What do you think?"

I hesitated. "When were you thinking?"

"These days I set my own schedule. You have a full-time job. You call it."

I looked at the clock and decided it was too late. "Tomorrow at Starbucks – either at 6 a.m. or 6 p.m.? As long as it doesn't rain. They have outdoor seating and Jasper likes it there."

"Let's go for the morning, then. And maybe some time you'll share how you've come to be so suspicious and careful. I have to say I'm impressed."

"In the morning then, and maybe some time you could fill in some blanks as well. Good night."

We disconnected and I wondered just how stupid it would be to get friendly with Kevin, a professional athlete with four unaccounted for years, who carries a gun and raises a host of other red flags.

I took extra care getting dressed the next morning, all the while reminding myself this was not a date and trying to impress Jasper with the importance of his role. He tilted his head at me and I laughed. When I grabbed his leash, he bounced around in circles.

I parked the car where I could easily see it. A few minutes early, I claimed one of the few tables on the patio. I watched as Kevin parked his car next to mine. I smiled when he got out of the car with a brown Labrador. That got Jasper's attention and he sat up on alert. I watched Kevin's expression as the realization my guard dog was a Maltese registered. He smiled back and shook his head.

"Not exactly ferocious, Stacie. Good morning to you and Jasper." He extended his hand and Jasper gave him a cursory sniff, his attention on the lab. "This here is Shaq."

"He's beautiful." I extended my hand and he responded with doggy kisses. "Let's see what happens." I put Jasper on the ground and they did the doggy dance. Shaq laid down in response to a hand signal from Kevin and Jasper followed suit. Who knew my dog was trained so well?

"He won't budge unless somebody bothers him. Skinny mocha, right? Anything else?"

I nodded and took Shaq's leash from him. "If they have a chocolate croissant, that would be great."

Kevin was right. Shaq barely moved. He lifted his head and stared into the store though, watching his master. Our timing was good, in between rushes, and Kevin was back in no time. As he sat back down, he prompted, "Tell me about your ferocious dog here. What's his story?"

"Jasper is a rescue. When I can find the time, I volunteer at Pet Connections, the local rescue. My… Ted stopped by one day and Jasper had just been surrendered. He was shaking and scared and I was trying to calm him. We adopted him as soon as he'd cleared the vet. What about Shaq? Did you find him in a shack?"

Kevin grimaced. "Shaq with a 'q' as in O'Neal?"

It was my turn to grimace. Of course, he'd name his dog after a basketball player. "Sorry, I wasn't thinking of basketball greats. Go on."

"Shaq found me. About six months ago I moved into this house. After a big rain storm, I was cleaning up the back yard and heard something. I investigated and found this puppy in the creek, floating on a log, whimpering, and hanging on for dear life. I got him out of the creek, posted notices, and in the meantime…" He shrugged. "He grew on me."

"That's a great story."

He took a sip of his coffee and his smile evaporated. "Stacie, I still don't get what's going on with the foundation. I get weird vibes from some of the people in the room. I can count the ones I trust on one hand."

"I know the feeling. Sometimes it seems very awkward, off. Then, I wonder if it's that I'm naïve."

"Like how?"

"For example, in my head, I would expect the Fire Chief and the Police Chief to work together and respect each other. Hang out together. They consistently sit about as far apart as possible. Rizzo talks to other people and so does Petkra, but not to each other. Rizzo seems okay. Petkra's never so much as acknowledged my presence."

"And then there's the animosity between the senators. You missed the argument and accusations going on after the other meeting. Petkra was in the middle of it before he talked with Stewart." He shook his head.

"That's interesting. Was it about the foundation? Whose side was he on?"

"Not about the foundation at all – gambling. Petkra agreed with Bryce that people who gambled would find a way – legal or not, in Virginia or not. Langford turned purple and argued all the obvious wrongs of legalized gambling. Chief Rizzo and I left them to it."

"What did you think of Dimbody? He was like out of the blue."

Jasper growled softly and then more emphatically. I glanced around and saw a man approach the Starbucks from the side street. The closer he got, the noisier Jasper got and nothing I did calmed him. Kevin moved quickly between the man and me.

He hissed, "Inside now."

I tried to grab Jasper and that was a no go. Kevin took a few steps toward the man as the man reached into his pocket. The man wasn't dumb, but he sure wasn't smart. Realizing that Kevin was onto him and bigger, he turned and tried to run. Kevin took off after him and I called the police. Man gone, Jasper calmed down, panting. Shaq tilted his head. The police cruiser arrived just as I spotted Kevin in the distance, returning with the man in tow, his arm pulled behind him. Rick shook his head as he and Flatt approached the table.

"Hey, Jasper. Did you get a new dog?"

"No, that's Shaq…" That's as far as I got before Jasper went crazy again.

Both Rick and Flatt stopped smiling. I shrugged and pointed to Kevin and the man.

"The man in the sweats was coming at us and Jasper didn't like it. Kevin stepped in and the man took off."

Jasper continued to growl and began to howl. "Can you please remove that man from Jasper's view?"

Flatt went over to where Kevin had stopped with the man and at least blocked Jasper's view. Within minutes, Flatt cuffed and put the man in the cruiser. Jasper calmed down and Kevin joined Rick and me.

"Talk to Kevin. I need to get Jasper some water."

I ducked into the Starbucks and let them introduce themselves. Of course, everyone in Starbucks had watched this whole incident and when I asked for a bowl of water, the barista was more than happy to comply.

"…drinking our coffee and talking about the foundation. I saw him but didn't give it much thought. I assumed he was just getting coffee like anyone else. Then Jasper… wow. I still wasn't sure. When he put his hand in his pocket, I wasn't taking any chances. I'm glad he at least had the safety on."

My mouth dropped. "Huh, what?"

Kevin changed the subject. "How did Jasper know he was a bad guy? He's not growling at Officer Murdock or Officer Flatt. He didn't growl at me."

I shrugged and smiled. "I don't know the answer to that, but after the last time he growled and went crazy, I'm not gonna question it."

With a wink and a smile, Rick explained, "And Jasper and me, we're buds."

Flatt interjected, "And we'll need to see that permit."

Kevin nodded and pulled out his wallet. Rick distracted me while McNair dealt with Flatt.

"We have McNair's version. Can you add anything?" He handed me his tablet with the report and I shook my head.

"If Jasper hadn't signaled danger, he probably would have mugged us."

Rick stared at me before he spoke. "Keep Jasper close by, Stacie. You seem to be a convenient target lately. You might want to think about who you're hanging out with."

I tilted my head and glared at him. McNair's glare matched mine as he caught Rick's comment.

"Hold on, that came out wrong. I didn't mean you, McNair. I meant the whole foundation thing. Something stinks about the whole thing."

I opened my mouth to speak and he held up his hand.

"I know Noth had the best of intentions and his heart was in the right place. I didn't mean to demean that either. At the same time, I doubt he intended you to have your car vandalized, someone try to break into your house twice, be shot at, or plant a tracker on your car. And now this."

Flatt cleared his throat. "Let's take this scumbag in and report to O'Hare."

Rick nodded. "Be careful and stay safe. Can't you resign from the foundation?" He nodded again, this time to Kevin, and followed Flatt to the car.

CHAPTER 19

I plopped back down in my chair, spent. Kevin picked up his cup and shook his head. "Let me get the dogs some more water and refills, okay?"

I nodded. He turned to go inside and turned around. With a wink, he added, "If your ferocious dog does his thing again, move this time, you hear."

I laughed and picked Jasper up and cuddled him. Shaq lifted his head and the upper part of his body. I leaned over and petted him. He obviously was not going to move. It dawned on me he never made a peep or moved the whole time Jasper was going nuts.

"What are you looking at Shaq like that for?" Kevin handed me a cup and filled the bowl with water before sitting down.

"You do realize that your puppy already outweighs Jasper and certainly could do more damage? You have him so well trained, he never moved. He never made a sound."

Kevin chuckled. "And I noticed you had to use your body weight to keep Jasper from taking off after that guy, and he weighs what? Ten pounds? Shaq is probably going to be a big boy, and I don't want to have to wrestle him if he wants to take off after someone or something. Right now, he barely notices the squirrels, but when he does, he chases them."

"Does he ever bark?"

"Not yet. He whimpered when he was hurt when I rescued him. He also hasn't had any role models to bark or growl – until now at least. I've kept him pretty much to myself and avoided dog parks and such."

"Any special reason?"

"Not all dog owners can control their dogs for one. Not all dog owners take good care of their dogs." He hesitated like there was something else, but didn't elaborate.

"Well, the only time Jasper barks, growls or howls, is when he senses something bad."

"And then he is ferocious." He laughed, then glanced away, then back.

"Murdock. You two have history?"

I squirmed. "I met Rick a couple weeks before my soon-to-be ex was murdered. I didn't know he was a cop until he and Flatt showed up at my house to tell me Ted was murdered. Needless to say, between our divorce papers and Ted's money, I was a suspect. Things got pretty complicated after that and when it was all over, Rick and I dated a couple of times."

He nodded and I continued. "He wanted the happily ever after and I … just not there yet. He's moved on."

"And you?"

"Me? I don't think I'm ready to jump into serious yet." I snickered. "I…"

He reached across the table and took my hand. "No worries. No pressure. Been there, done that."

I lifted my head and got lost in those blue eyes. "Done what?"

He chuckled, but it was hollow. "Married too young. Didn't last long. Neither of us had a clue how much work goes into the happily ever after."

I nodded.

***

I called Jillian and told her I was running late, and I'd drive myself. I had a text message from Nate, short but to the point. "Smythe is one of the good guys."

It was a quiet day at work and I managed to get there almost on time. I needed to finish the quarter end reports for Reinhardt or she would be on my case. I'd checked in on Kayla Anderson once this week already; she was doing as well as could be expected.

My friends and I did a salad lunch and chatted about work. Ronnie shared more pictures of Elle, and Trina talked about Bill. The usual questions about my life hadn't come up yet when Smythe called.

"Hello, Stacie? Lionel Smythe here."

"Hi, Mr. Smythe." My friends stopped talking and watched me.

"Can you spare some time after work for a meeting?"

"What's the issue?"

"Jacob and I have been going through all the emails. It ends up Trichter really did give a list to Langford. Beasley and the Kearns fellow were on that list. There's also documentation that you suggested Shawna Jackson and Dr. Sarah Hanreddy. Then it gets … 'squirrelly' is the best

I can describe it. I need your help to sort out what happened after that."

"I could meet you at 6 o'clock, but please not the Fried Tomato." Smythe, as well as my friends listening to the conversation, all burst out laughing.

"How about the pizza place on Main? Will that work?"

"Much better. I'll see you then."

As soon as I hung up, Ronnie asked, "Why does he need your help? Are you sure he's safe?"

"Nate checked him out and said he was okay. From talking to him, this is not the usual foundation business he's used to dealing with. Something weird is going on. Even Kevin mentioned it this morning…" I stopped, realizing I hadn't even told Jillian I was meeting up with Kevin or shared the incident with the menacing man.

"What happened this morning? With Kevin?" Jillian sat forward.

"We met at Starbucks and some man would have mugged us, except for Jasper. He warned us and Kevin chased the guy and caught him. That's why I was late. After the police arrested the man, I needed to decompress."

Ronnie's mouth dropped. Jillian waved her arms.

"What! Stacie, what is going on?"

"I don't know." I didn't mention that the man was carrying and so was Kevin.

Trina asked the magic question with a twinkle in her eye. "So, which of Beckman Springs' finest responded?"

"Not Bill." I groaned. "Rick and Flatt."

Trina laughed and Jillian shook her head.

Ronnie asked, "Was your life always this chaotic?"

"Nope. Except for the chaos on my desk. I need to get some work done so I can get out of here on time and take care of Jasper before meeting up with Smythe."

The pizza place was crowded when I got there. Smythe had arrived early and snagged a booth. He was making notes as I approached the table.

"Hi, Mr. Smythe. Busy place. How are you doing?"

He smiled and pushed the pad of paper to the side. "Hi, Stacie. Good, good. What shall we order? Are you good with sausage and peppers?"

"That sounds great. Are those notes all related to the foundation?"

"They are. Let's get the pizza ordered and then I've tried – emphasis on 'tried' – to make some sense of all this. Here, you can read these. I'd be interested in hearing what you think."

The waitress came and he placed the order. I scanned the emails and wished for a highlighter. Phrases like "I'm sure you understand the importance, Will, of heeding my advice in handling foundation funds" coupled with "Remind me to show you those pictures I took – I'll have to share them with you the next time we get together" could be innocuous or sinister.

Each email to the Senator had a similar comment along with statements asking about the Senator's family and his daughter, Meredith. All mentioned the Noth Foundation in passing and all were unsigned. The Senator's response to more than one of them indicated he'd pass on the information to his staffer, Patsy Andrus. He never mentioned the other two staffers.

I looked up at Smythe after reading the four email threads he'd shared. "Definitely ambiguous enough. Potentially a threat depending on what those photos are of and how close this person is to the Langford family and Meredith. Odd there's no signature."

Smythe nodded. "Therein lies the problem. Here are two more and here's our pizza. *Mange.*"

"*Buon appetito.*"

These two were a little more pointed, yet still ambiguous. One read:

> Thanks, Will, for contacting me about possible members of your new board. I'll check around and see who I can come up with. In the meantime, you mentioned two people – Stewart and Maroni as stipulated by Noth. Not sure of his reasoning, but with their obvious connection to Noth, they could make it difficult for you to effectively serve as Chairman of the Board. Maroni could be a thorn in your side. After all, she didn't inherit that half mil. Stewart is a little too savvy and has a big ego. Maybe you could suggest they decline the invitation to be on the board. Otherwise, you could have a power struggle there. You shouldn't take any chances, you need to hedge your bets.

"Again, ambiguous, but given all that's happened to both Stewart and me..." At Smythe's dropped jaw, I shared what Stewart had told me.

The next one suggested Dimbody, Petkra, Senator Bryce, and a few names I'd never heard of as good people to have on the Board. Whoever this person was, he or she was obviously aware of the stakeholders to be identified and commented, "For the first responders, I'd go with Petkra over Rizzo if I were you – he's more manageable. Remember, we saw him that night in Hanover?"

I shrugged as the reference to Hanover didn't make any sense to me. I ate my pizza and waited for my next installment from the stack.

Smythe nodded. "Here's a few more that went directly to Ms. Andrus, but the salutation is to Langford."

One email stated the obvious that membership on the board needed to be determined in ways that seemed legit. The message suggested Petkra along with Stewart and Langford do the vetting. That was followed by a question: "How is Meredith doing these days? Maybe I should give her a call."

I hesitated and didn't say anything, but recalled that Meredith and Ted became involved after she was a victim herself. Was that a veiled threat from her abuser? Or a solicitous comment by a family friend.

The next couple of emails maligned first Beasley and then McNair, with a comment, "A few missed meetings and you can get rid of them I'm sure. Your work with the NFL aside, there are those with concerns about betting in sports."

I glanced back through all the emails. Whether to Langford or through the same staffer no other identifying information other than the email address and that was always different. I wondered if the person could even receive emails at these addresses or if they could be tracked. ABCD [at] and some [dot] com or net didn't provide any indication of the sender's identity.

I remembered a friend telling me how he avoided spam email by generating a random email address each time he entered a contest. He had it linked to his main account and weekly would go through and delete those accounts as soon as the contests ended. Anyone sending an email to that address would get a delivery failure message.

Ned had received many of these emails as well, and in at least one instance, he forwarded the email to Langford with a question about the propriety of the content and someone not on the board making pointed suggestions about who should be invited. Maybe that's what got him killed. As if reading my mind, Smythe handed me another email – the last one from Ned to Langford.

> Senator, I think you need to call a meeting. I fear the integrity of the foundation is at risk. There are significant inconsistencies between the incorporation papers and who is included on the emails, for example. I feel strongly that legal counsel should be involved, yet Mr. Smythe is not included in many of the emails between you and your staffers or me. Please, call an emergency meeting of the board at your earliest convenience. Please be sure that all parties are invited.

For a young man moonlighting as the admin, Ned had integrity and took his job seriously. Too bad that worked against him. We finished our pizza. Smythe still had a few emails he hadn't shared.

"Can't you do something from a legal perspective?"

"Unfortunately, it is all too subtle. There's not enough to charge anyone and all is offered as opinion, even if we knew who it was. There is no clear threat to Langford, you, Stewart, or me. And, yes, I am mentioned in a few emails as well. My good reputation and extensive experience with non-profits are a little worrisome for whoever this is. Chief Rizzo turned all this over to one of his detectives. I'm guessing it will get put on a back burner with no explicit threat, yet he wants all of this on file in relation to Ned Anderson's murder, just in case." Smythe shrugged.

"So, what are you holding back?"

He smiled. "Surprise, surprise. The same person I suspect, email address ABCD [at] rusticroad [dot] net is the recipient of the grant — though there are no procedures in place and no proposal and he or she is not identified by name."

He handed me an email from Langford congratulating him or her on the award for $100,000. It didn't say what the money was to be used for or anything resembling what a grant award would look like. It was an original email, not part of a chain. There was no indication that the email had been received. I stared at him speechless.

"Do you know that this person actually received this email? The address looks bogus to me.

"Langford confirmed he sent the email and has now informed the grantee – who he did not choose to identify – that there is a delay."

I stared at him and he shrugged his shoulders again. "I asked to see the grant proposal and Langford smiled and assured me everything was in order and he'd prefer not to make the award public until the appropriate time as it was politically sensitive, whatever that means."

My mouth dropped.

Smythe nodded. "The staffer, Ms. Andrus, must have wondered, but there's no indication she said anything and she did include all the emails in the batch to Jacob."

"Maybe she forgot they were in the batch or this seemed perfectly normal to her?"

Smythe shook his head. "Hard to tell. I'm not sure the detective on Ned's case has talked to any of the staffers, least of all, Ms. Andrus. Also, lots of secrets and deals in politics. Often senators agree to vote for a bill someone else wanted so they can then get the swing vote on a bill that's in their best interest. Happens all the time. And then there's all the lobbyists."

Neither of us had anything else to say. The whole situation was convoluted. Definitely, if this was what was involved in politics, none of them should look cross-eyed when it came to coercion and pressuring people to do what they wanted. Smythe picked up the check with a comment about the expense account and we parted ways.

After a quiet afternoon at work, I reflected on the lunch conversation. My initial attempt to see how often Senators Langford and Bryce voted at odds with each other wasn't very fruitful. I found one reference to a heated argument between them over whether gambling and casinos should be allowed in Virginia. From the video clip that popped up, Langford was saying no and Bryce was arguing that a lottery was gambling and already legal. She called him pompous and the clip ended. Maybe Wade or Jillian would know more, or Smythe.

I admitted to myself I was glad Kevin's name didn't show up in any of the emails Smythe had shared as suspicious. It didn't sound like whoever was behind the email trail wanted him or Beasley on the board. I detoured to Yoga Pod for a quick thirty minutes and then went home to Jasper.

My tracker sweeper arrived and I played with it. As far as I could tell, there was no tracker on my car. It did bleep near the alarm system. That made sense to me in some warped way – the security company and the camera systems were tracking me and relaying information electronically.

CHAPTER 20

As we'd planned earlier in the week, Jillian, Wade, and I went to Rockies. Rockies was at the end of a strip mall and the doors opened from the end rather than parallel to the other businesses. It opened late in the afternoon and food-wise was best known for barbecue. Things didn't start hopping until the weekend and the after-dinner crowd. Sometimes there was a live band, other times a DJ.

The parking lot wasn't crowded, but nine o'clock was early for a Friday night. I could hear the music and recognized a song by Journey as we entered. Lighting was low enough to set a romantic mood. As Wade led us to a table near the dance floor, I glanced around. A mixed crowd with some of the dancers very young and one or two easily in their sixties.

"See the older man dancing his heart out?"

I nodded to Jillian and she continued. "He's a fixture here. He loves to dance and is always looking for a partner, so you better watch out."

I laughed and slid down in my seat.

"We can only hope to have that much energy when we're his age. Anything new with your foundation fiasco?"

"Actually, Wade, maybe you could help me out. In addition to Senator Langford, there's another Senator – Clarisse Bryce – on the board. They don't seem to get along. I tried to figure out if they were adversaries politically, you know, voting against each other or if they had a *quid pro quo* thing going on. Any ideas?"

"My opinion? Not facts, mind you. Langford says what he thinks people want to hear and votes the way he's pressured to regardless of what he says. Bryce is a whole other story. She's a bully of sorts and doesn't really care who she runs over if they're in the way of her getting what she feels she's earned or she's worked toward. As a black man? Sometimes I agree with her agenda. Sometimes, I think she misses the boat."

"So, do they vote the same way? Or oppose each other?"

He chuckled. "Each might be swayed if it suited their purposes. With Bryce, she'd have to think it was her idea though."

"Any issues in particular where they oppose each other?"

"Gambling. There's been a long battle in Virginia about allowing casinos. Other than the occasional charity casino night, there's only the river boat and the track. And, of course, the lottery. Langford preaches – and I do mean preaches – of the ills of gambling. Bryce takes the practical response that people who gamble will gamble anyway and until Virginia gets in the game, pun intended, people are going to other places and effectively Virginia is giving away the money they lose."

"So, she wants Virginians to lose their shirt in Virginia, not Maryland? And he wanted to keep gambling out of Virginia?"

"You got it. Recently the bill passed – over Langford's rather loud protests. That makes it a moot point. I watched some of the hearings and debates. That's the only time they disagreed in a public forum I know of."

His expression changed and he grimaced. "Stacie, any idea why your detective friend would be here?"

"What? No idea."

I turned to follow Wade's line of sight, and sure enough, O'Hare was at the bar and waved at us. Beer in hand, he walked over and sat down.

"Nice place here. I've never been before." The DJ switched to an Eagles tune, and O'Hare smiled. "DJ or somebody has good taste."

We all stared at him and I finally blurted out, "Why are you here, why choose to try out Rockies tonight?"

"And there I was trying to be sociable." He paused before he continued. "I stopped at The Brick. Trina told me you three were checking out Rockies tonight."

I nodded, not sure whether to strangle Trina or thank her. He took a swig of his beer and scanned the area around us. Somehow, I didn't get the feeling this was a social call.

The music stopped and the DJ announced, "Tonight, by popular demand, we will have karaoke on the hour for three songs. If you're interested, sign up with Marty at the bar. Now, a little Carrie Underwood."

Wade moaned and Jillian burst out laughing. O'Hare's eyebrows raised, he looked at me.

"It was only once. I had too much to drink. I can't help it if I'm tone deaf."

O'Hare looked at Wade. "That bad?"

Wade and Jillian both nodded and Jillian added, "Just keep her away from the microphone."

We all laughed. The conversation was easy after that and O'Hare and I even danced a few times, which kept the elderly dancer from picking on me to fill his dance card. Mostly, O'Hare talked to Wade while Jillian and I chatted about nothing. I noticed both of them scanning the bar continuously. Probably a function of their professions. I wasn't too sure.

"Did you ever figure out what was going on in that interview with McNair?" O'Hare asked Wade when the DJ took a break and it was quiet enough for conversation.

"I watched a copy of the tape. Blake started off asking what seemed like reasonable questions. How did McNair feel about his stats, the team, his future – pretty much what you'd expect. He gave the polished responses he's been trained to give. Then she asked about his free agent status and suggested his career was over. He handled that well, acknowledging that each time he found himself in that position, he considered a change in careers and he'd see how it all played out."

"That's expected. What happened then?"

"It didn't make much sense actually, which made it harder for him to respond on the spot. Blake twisted what he said about a career change and instead of going with the usual coaching jobs or something sports related, she asked him if being on the board for the foundation would pay him as well as playing basketball. He hesitated, which was his downfall, and tried to explain that being on the board was a volunteer activity, that he wouldn't get paid. She accused him of having an ulterior and nefarious motive, and pointed to his hesitation in responding to his question. He was blindsided and she ran all over him for the last few minutes with a smile on her face."

"That's a bit bizarre, don't you think? Was her intent to discredit him."

"Oh, yeah. No doubt about it."

I'd listened to their conversation and had to ask, "For what purpose?"

Wade rubbed his chin, his head tilted. "Two possibilities. One, to make him less desirable in the draft to up the odds for someone who's competing with him for a slot."

He shrugged and continued. "Two, to malign the foundation and the good it could do."

"You spending a lot of time with him, Stacie? Has he been to your house?" Unsaid, O'Hare's expression and tone had a negative edge.

"No, he's never been to my house – at least not that I know of. He's on the board for the foundation. We had coffee one morning. No big deal." Without a doubt, O'Hare already knew about the arrest at the Starbucks.

He nodded. "It's getting late folks. I'm out of here. Thanks for letting me crash your party."

As he left, Jillian turned to Wade. "What was that all about?" Wade shrugged, but didn't make eye contact and his next comment was an attempt to divert the conversation.

"We had enough yet? I'm not sure but it seems like nobody doing karaoke can sing tonight."

We all laughed. At the house, Wade checked the security system. When I commented on his concern, he commented on the number of accidents and bad karma I'd been experiencing. I showed him my tracking sweeper and he guffawed.

"Hey, so far no one's connected the Hilton fire with the foundation meeting. In fact, the foundation hasn't been in the news for several days. And, thankfully, there's been no word from Langford. And I heard the Heart Association is hosting a casino night tomorrow…"

"Really? Shall we go?" Jillian smiled and looked to Wade.

"I don't think we have other plans."

"Okay. That's settled." Wade studied his feet for a few seconds, then made eye contact. "Stacie, I know what your response will be. I'm going to suggest it anyway and I know I'm not the first. For your own well-being, you may want to separate yourself from the foundation and Langford. Do your own thing to support victims and develop better prevention programs."

I didn't say a word, no idea what to say.

Jillian finally broke the silence. "Think about it. Sleep on it. Stay safe."

With Jasper in my arms, I set the alarm once they had left.

CHAPTER 21

Saturday is supposed to be my day to sleep in, yet my phone woke me up. I answered before it registered that CallerID said "unknown number" instead of my father or Nate or Jillian.

"Hello."

"Good morning, Ms. Maroni. This is Barbie Blake of KCAM Channel 10. How are you this morning?"

I sat up and stared at the phone and recoiled from the way too perky voice. "I'm fine, Ms. Blake."

"Good, good. I'm calling to invite you to be my guest on my talk show this week. It would be great publicity for you and your late husband's legacy foundation. I understand how important it is to you to see his dreams carried out."

She certainly had a way with words and guilt, and her voice was smooth as silk. "I'm sorry, Ms. Blake, I have no interest in being on your... Excuse me, what was that beeping sound?"

"Oh, we have to record all our calls. Just documentation to show that we're on the job, you know. Don't you worry about it now."

"Ms. Blake, as I started to say, I have no interest in being on your show."

"Well, perhaps you'd be willing to answer a few questions for me. I'm particularly interested in the fire at the Hilton and Kevin McNair's appointment to the foundation board. Isn't that a conflict of interest?"

Very glad she couldn't see my glaring face, I smiled and spoke softly, on purpose. "Ms. Blake, any questions you have about the foundation should be directed to the Chairman, Senator Langford."

"But surely, you could answer just a few questions without his permission."

"Nice try, Ms. Blake. I'm sure you can find his number on his website. Good day."

I disconnected and stared at the phone. My number was unlisted, so how did she even get my number to call me? Jasper hit my hand with his nose and I realized I was getting up whether I liked it or not.

Jasper taken care of and coffee in hand, I called Mr. Smythe.

"Hi, Mr. Smythe, Stacie here. How are you?"

"Good. What's up?"

"I was wondering if you gave out our phone numbers or if there was some record of all the board member phone numbers."

"Not that I know of. Senator Langford provided me with a list. That's how I had your number to call you. Same with everyone else. Why do you ask?"

"That talk show host? Barbie Blake? She called me and invited me to be on her show and talk about the foundation. I have an unlisted number so I'm trying to figure out how she got it."

He groaned. "Not good. I suspect that the staffers had the same list I was provided. Any one of them could have provided her with the list or your number if she asked for it."

"That's not the worst. She made the connection between the foundation and the fire at the Hilton. She mentioned it."

"What did you tell her?"

"Nothing. Well, actually, I told her to contact Senator Langford. You might want to run some interference and suggest he not talk to her."

"I doubt he'll listen, but I'll give it a shot. Thanks for the heads up, Stacie."

After I disconnected, I picked up around the house and got the laundry going. That was one advantage to getting up early – I could get household chores done before going out to Cornerstone.

I ate and decided to once again try to find how Langford and Bryce had voted on legislation over the past year. It wasn't easy but Google came through and found a site for Langford's voting record. I created an excel sheet and listed each bill, the date, and his vote. Then I did the same for Bryce.

I sat back and looked at it. Historically, they had only voted the same way on two bills, both having to do with disaster relief. Then something changed, and more recently, they voted the same way. I pulled up Langford's webpage and read his positions on the various bills that had come up recently. He'd voted in opposition to his stated position. Very odd indeed. I ruminated on it as I dressed and left.

***

A pleasant fall day, not yet cold and no longer too hot, I pulled my hair back into a messy bun and drove with the windows open. It gave me a feeling of freedom and for the short time it took to get to Cornerstone, I focused on the beauty around me. Shawna and Layla were both in the office when I arrived.

"Morning, ladies. How're things here?

Layla commented, "Not too hectic, but you know violence tends to go in cycles and is often precipitated by stress. No major lay-offs or economic issues and no holidays? A little bit of relief."

She was right. The incidence of domestic violence and child abuse increased around holidays, possibly fueled by both family tension and the abundance of alcohol, as well as when the economy tanked and families were stressed out. Both of those factors likely contributed to the excuses made by victims. Unfortunately, not all domestic violence followed that pattern – for some, it was their release after a bad day, any day.

"A new woman arrived last night, but she's not ready to talk to anyone yet. Not in bad shape physically – only a couple broken ribs. Traumatized enough though. I'm guessing for her, this is the first and last time she'll be a punching bag."

Shawna nodded and smiled. Then she added, "And we've made progress with Princess Why."

"Really? That's great."

Shaking her head, Shawna explained, "So far, if she's telling the truth, she answered an ad for a modeling job and when she showed up, the people who interviewed her were very nice and gave her a glass of iced tea. She doesn't remember much else until she woke up in a warehouse with a bunch of other girls. She still won't tell us her name. She did tell the police the address of the office she went to for the interview and the area in Reston where the warehouse was. The police in that jurisdiction are searching the area and checking missing persons. They hope to identify her soon…"

"What about Princess Vi?"

"Princess Vi is conscious but not speaking. Physically she is doing much better… not so emotionally. She is completely shut down."

"They came in together. Did they know each other before this happened to them?"

Shawna shrugged. "Two days ago, Princess Why moved herself into Princess Vi's room. She talks to her some, but mostly reads to her. As far as we can tell, no response."

"And the others?"

"Pretty much what you'd expect. Two women left. One didn't go home, but went to some relatives and filed charges against her husband. I cheered for her. The other one? She made excuses as she has consistently since she's been here. She was sure he would change and she didn't feel she had much of a choice."

Layla, another survivor who worked at Cornerstone snorted. "The irony? The smart one? She had very little money and resources, and she's gonna have a tough time finding a new job and starting over. The one who went back to the abusive relationship? She had enough spending money on her to go anywhere she wanted. She even offered to pay for her stay."

"That's probably a first. We know the cycle and do all we can to break it. Sad. Enough of the melancholy. I'll check in with the princesses and the others and see if I can help crack the armor a little."

Shawna was right about Princess Why. She was dressed in shorts and a t-shirt, both loose on her. Her long blonde hair was brushed, and most of the bruising had disappeared. She was open to talking about what happened and like all victims, she'd taken on some of the blame.

"I should have known getting a modeling job wouldn't be that easy. I should have taken someone with me as a watch dog. Never should have drank the iced tea they offered."

"Were there other girls there, waiting to be interviewed?"

"A few. When I called they gave me an appointment time. Said it was important to be prompt. There were two other girls and a receptionist. The receptionist said something about the interviews running late. One of the other girls was called in and then my name was called. It was a nice office. I remember thinking the other girls were so pretty and better dressed, I didn't have a chance."

"Did you ever see them again?"

She shrugged. "All the girls were pretty, blonde, and fair, though. At least one of those girls was a brunette." She choked out, "I guess she didn't get the job. Probably doesn't know how lucky she was."

"And this young lady?" At Princess Why's request, we were talking in the room with Princess Vi and I could tell she was listening.

"We were sent to the same house. They dressed us up..." She trembled and I waited. "The man... he was mean. I felt so helpless and couldn't fight back. I passed out. Next thing I knew we were here."

She started to cry and I rubbed her arm. Princess Vi started to cry, too, and I heard her whisper, "Tam."

Winging it, I said, "Tam? How about we move closer to your friend's bed?"

She didn't correct me and scooted her chair over and I did the same.

"No one can make what happened go away. It's important to talk about it, heal as best you can, and move on. First physically and then emotionally. Shawna, Layla, and even the other women will help you."

They both nodded. "I'll be back next Saturday and someone else will be in during the week."

I spoke to a few of the other women, including the newest arrival. Mostly words of hope and support. In the office, I let Shawna know that Princess Why might at least have a first name or nickname – Tam.

"And Shawna, these two are out of my league. They're kids and more traumatized. You'll need to find someone better trained than me."

Shawna nodded. "We already have someone on standby. I'll give them the word to come on over if you think they're ready."

I nodded. "At least Tam is, and Princess Vi at least responded to our talk. Too bad there isn't someone on standby to fix this foundation fiasco."

"You've got that right, girl. Dr. Hanreddy and I were talking and that is one odd bunch starting with Langford himself. What is he on anyway?"

"I don't know." I grimaced. "I never considered his stupidity and attitude to be drug-induced – certainly a possibility. Though, given what we hear from most politicians, I envision some class they take where they learn to dodge the truth, smile while they tell you falsehoods, make you miserable, and try to make you feel like you should like it."

"Yeah, I'd believe that. And Bryce? She is one scary lady. I heard her and Langford going at it. That combination is volatile and Langford is going to lose the battle. You still having all those coincidental bad things happening?"

"Not in the last 24 hours, knock on wood." I moved to the wooden table and knocked for good measure. Not that I'm superstitious, but no point in tempting fate.

"Interesting thing I discovered this morning. Recently, Langford is voting with Bryce – on everything."

The two women stared at me. Dr. Hanreddy was the first to react. "That's crazy. It may explain his behavior. What do you think is going on?"

"I don't know. As far as I can tell he is diametrically opposed to her. It makes no sense. Sometimes I just don't understand people."

Shawn shook her head. "Stacie, you figured out if you're going back to school? Getting that additional training so you can understand and explain them to us?"

"I may get some additional training. Not so sure about the degree. Still thinking about it."

"And what are you thinking about the blue-eyed jock?" Shawna winked. "And what's with his chummy relationship with the chief of police?"

I shrugged. "Not sure on those either. Kevin McNair is great eye candy, yet he's almost too good to be true. His sudden chumminess with the chief is a red flag to me. I'm not sure what his story is and can't quite trust him." I took a deep breath and added, "One on one though, I like him. And I saw your reaction to Austin Beasley…"

Shawna laughed as the phone rang. She gave me a quick hug. "See you at the next meeting of misfits or next Saturday."

CHAPTER 23

Jasper and I spent the afternoon at the park with Ronnie and Elle again. Before long it would be too cold to hang out at a picnic table, but right now it was just right. Elle fell asleep on a blanket, Jasper by her side.

"Stacie, I always wondered how you and Ted met. Did you get involved in trauma counseling because of him or is that how you met?"

I chuckled. "Those would be two likely explanations. Only neither is quite correct." I looked off to the trees before I answered.

"I'm from a small family, only one brother, four years younger than me, Vince. Both my parents worked most of the time when I was growing up. Neither of my parents went to college, they were blue collar all the way. My dad worked and still works construction. My mom worked in the business office at a construction company. That's how they met."

I sighed. "College was not really in the picture. Teachers and counselors at school kept telling me I needed to go to college. I was able to get a scholarship, so I went. It was hard in many ways, but mostly because I had no clue and limited experience. That's when I met Jillian and we became friends."

I stopped to guzzle some water. "Anyway, I started off thinking I'd go into accounting or business. Jillian and I hung out with a few other girls. One of them was raped my freshman year. Someone else I knew? Her sister was beat up by a boyfriend. A bunch of us pushed to get self-defense classes offered and took them. One of the teachers mentioned the need for social workers to help victims recover and regain their lives. I finished all the accounting classes and took psychology classes initially as electives. Ended up with a double major BA in Social Work and in Business. Odd combination."

"That is an odd combination, but it obviously works for you."

"It does, in many ways. My senior year, I did an internship at Recovery Services – it later became Cornerstone. That's how I met Ted. At one of the banquets to raise money for the project though, not at the shelter. I had no idea who he was in the social scheme of things and didn't care. We dated and the rest is history."

"So, it was your shared interest that brought you together. And I've gathered from the lunch conversations you planned to continue your education before you married Ted?"

"That was the plan – get my Masters in Social Work. Ted's father felt it was more important that I be a wife in the traditional sense, at least in the country club context. It was okay to do volunteer work, but no need to get a degree. Education for a woman? A waste of time. My parents didn't have strong feelings one way or the other. It ended up, my aunt was battered and my mom was proud of what I was doing. I don't think either of them understood why I'd need another degree though."

"Didn't Mr. Noth have a problem with your working at Foster's?"

I chuckled. "Hamilton Noth is a Neanderthal. He had me sign a prenup and then took every precaution to make sure I couldn't access any of the Noth money. I tried doing the country club stuff. It wasn't me, I was miserable, and besides, I had student loans to pay off. His father refused to allow Ted to pay off my loans, so when they came due, I got a job. By then, my mom was ill and my dad couldn't afford the medical bills and help me with my loans. If my working was a blemish on the family name, it was just too bad. Ted got it. Mr. Noth never did. To him? I'm just white trash and always will be."

"I'm sorry. It's not the same I know, yet similar. I'm the fair-skinned red head among the Gomez family and I'm still trying to learn Spanish so I can understand what they're saying. I often feel like the outsider. Elle here serves as bridge though my parents and Andy's parents don't do well in the same room for very long."

"Yeah. I can see where that might be awkward."

"What about your brother?"

"By the time I graduated, my brother enlisted in the army. He's making that his career and we have little contact with him except when he's on leave. Usually, Vince goes to New York to see my dad though, not down here. He drops a line once in a while, but we're definitely not close."

"Will you go back to school?"

"Maybe. I don't know. Foster's is comfortable right now – the only thing that hasn't changed in the past year. What I may do is some professional development and see where it takes me."

"I think that's a great idea. I'd actually like to get some more training as well."

Elle chose that moment to start screaming and Jasper jumped. We both laughed and moved at the same time.

"Maybe when she's in kindergarten…"

Jasper and I napped after lunch and then I dressed for the Heart Association Casino Night. It was at the country club and that crowd always intimidated me. There would be any number of physicians, lawyers, politicians, and the social elite, along with the rest of us who were willing to donate a hundred dollars for a few hours entertainment to support a good cause.

On the plus side, there would be food and drink and fun, and maybe my friends and dad would stop bugging me about getting out. Wade, once again, played the designated driver. He had done so ever since he met Jillian and she shared stories of our wilder days and precarious drives home. The country club was decorated with hearts galore. Parking was valet only tonight and Jillian's Accord was no match for the fancy cars in line ahead of us. The valet shook his head at us.

We paid for our tickets and entered the "casino" in the main ballroom. I heard music from one of the smaller ballrooms where there were often private parties. In all the years Ted and I were married, we never attended casino nights so I hoped not to see his parents. I'd always felt I was invisible unless Ted was by my side when I was here. Tonight, invisible would be good.

"I see some slot machines. That's where I'm going. What about you guys?"

"I like slots too. We have the credits to play for a while. How about a drink first, Stacie?"

"Sounds good. Wade?"

Wade tilted his head to the craps table. "I'll be over there. Let me know when you've had enough."

Needless to say, the slot machines were hungry and it didn't take long for me to feed them all hundred credits or to finish my glass of wine. Jillian, on the other hand, held her own.

"I'm gonna walk around and make my way to the restroom. You want anything?"

"Another glass of wine would be good. Don't get lost now."

I pretend punched her in the arm and meandered through the tables to the hallway. I passed a few people I recognized and smiled, just in case. As usual, there were a couple of ladies in the restroom, and either I truly was invisible or they didn't care who heard their conversation.

"Pretty calm here tonight. Not like at the Casino in Hanover last weekend."

"That was intense. Did you ever find out who they were?"

"Sure did. My friend's friend works security there. She said he said it's happened before. I thought it was the senator with the problem, but no. Apparently Monica Langford has a gambling problem, a big gambling problem, and she drinks. He tries to keep her away from the tables, but sometimes she manages despite his efforts and he shows up to drag her out. No telling how much she's lost."

"I bet that's why he was so opposed to legalizing gambling in Virginia. She made quite the spectacle that night. How embarrassing for him."

"He's just lucky the media hasn't picked up on it."

I washed my hands as they finished their conversation and left. Obviously, there was something to be said for being invisible.

Stopping at the bar for two glasses of wine, I was surprised when someone tapped on my shoulder. Turning around, I was surprised to see Nate.

"Hi Nate. I didn't know you'd be here. How are you?"

"I'm doing well and you're looking good, Stacie. I don't often frequent this place, but with so many of my clients of a certain age, I support all the Heart Association does. You here by yourself?"

"With Wade and Jillian." The bartender handed me the two glasses of wine. "Wine is for Jillian and me. Wade's over at the craps table. Always the craps table."

"My kind of man. You ladies must be at the slots, right?" He leaned in and lowered his voice. "With your memory and math skills, you should try Black Jack or poker. At least it would challenge you more than pushing the button on the slots. I'll go say hello to Wade."

He turned to leave and then came back. "You got my texts on your legal counsel, right? Smythe's top notch, well-respected. Catch you later."

I chuckled at his back, picked up our wines went in search of Jillian. She and Wade both finished playing with their credits about the same time and we all agreed, sleep was in order.

CHAPTER 23

My phone rang while I was eating breakfast on Sunday.

"Hi, Stacie. You got a minute?"

"Hi, Kevin. Yeah, I got a minute. What's on your mind?"

I heard him exhale and waited.

"Langford is an idiot. Big time. He made the mistake of agreeing to do an interview with Barbie Blake. She called and invited me in case he brings up my motives – so I have a chance to defend myself, she said. I declined."

"That's good. That you declined, I mean. She called me, too. I declined as well. I can't figure out how she got my number though. It's unlisted. But wait – how did you get my number?" I heard my voice and paranoia rising and worked at tamping both down.

"The night someone tried to break into your house. You called to let me know you were safe."

"That's right. But I never called her."

"Well, I sure didn't give out your number. I wouldn't wish her on anyone, not even Langford. Blake will tear him to shreds. Doesn't he have people to advise him better."

"I don't know. I think Smythe was going to talk to him in case she called. Do you know when this interview will happen? It's live, right?"

"Yes. It's live but also recorded and parts often used as fillers in other broadcasts. Often out of context. He is in so much trouble."

I shared with him my imagined class politicians must take. "Maybe he'll out finesse and dance around her."

He laughed. "You say that like a joke. Not necessarily formal or a class, still, there is coaching in dealing with the media for athletes, particularly at the pro level. Anyway, to answer your question, the show with Langford is set for Thursday evening at half past six. Shall we watch the slaughter together?"

I hesitated. "Where?"

"Your place? Jasper would be there. My place and Shaq? Some place neutral and we can stream it?"

He was doing it again. Giving me choices. I hesitated and made a decision. "My place. With Jasper for sure." And, hopefully, Jillian and Wade.

"Great. In the meantime, care to meet me at the park, maybe for a run this evening when it cools down?"

"Sure." I gave him the address, disconnected, and called Jillian to see if I could stop over.

At Jillian's, I was immediately attacked by her cat, Meow. Wade pulled her off me and Jillian gave me a hug.

"What's up?"

"I just need to talk with my friends – too many issues and questions keep floating into my head."

Wade set his jaw. "That foundation thing again? A bunch of rich folks flexing their money so they don't have to feel guilty."

We'd had this conversation before and I didn't take the bait this time. "Ted had the best of intentions here. Other nonprofits can't have this level of impaired communication. Certainly not what I envisioned."

"I've never given it any thought. What did you envision?"

I answered Jillian's question while Wade went to grab some beers. "I envisioned we'd come up with a template for a proposal to do "something" – public education, prevention activities like self-defense training, better access to mental health professionals with trauma training."

Wade handed me a beer. "That would be the normal process. And then there'd be a review of proposals and funds committed until there wasn't any more to award that year. That's how it is supposed to work."

"But it's a mess – a hot mess. Really."

They both nodded and Wade took a chance on the silence. "When are you getting off the foundation, cutting loose from the Noths?"

"Once it gets off the ground. Then I won't feel guilty, like I'm letting him down somehow."

About to continue, I was distracted by a call from Smythe. "Stacie, are you available Wednesday evening? I've convinced Langford we need to have a practice interview."

"That's a good idea. Blake is brutal. What's the plan?"

"I want you to brainstorm some questions she might throw at him. I've studied a few of her interviews and she has a definite pattern. You'll have to get some history on some of his accomplishments so he can preen. That'll get him relaxed. Then, we can take turns asking questions about those odd emails and maybe the hostility with Bryce?"

"Good idea. It's very possible she got wind of those or even managed to get a copy. She obviously got my phone number from someone in his office."

"Can you get off work early? I want to be in and out of there before the building empties out and while security is there."

"That sounds reasonable. I can work through lunch and leave at four, be at Langford's office by half past four. Will that give us enough time?"

"It should." I disconnected and shared the conversation, the interview with Langford, and the game plan Smythe had come up with.

"He's right. Blake will eat him alive and spit him out. He won't know what hit him."

"And it won't have to be foundation-based either. I did some checking and all of a sudden Langford is voting with Bryce, in opposition of his own positions."

Wade worked his jaw. "Let me see what I can find out. Something is rotten here, and you're right, it's not just about the foundation."

I leaned back, opened my mouth and then closed it.

"Okay, Stacie, what else is on your mind?"

"First, a favor. Can you guys come over to my place to watch the interview on Thursday? Kevin is coming over."

Wade scowled and Jillian smiled. "I knew you liked him."

Wade followed up with, "Just be careful, Stacie. You said 'first' – is there a 'second'?"

"Umm, now that you ask, I agreed to go running with him at the park this evening. Is that stupid?"

Wade hesitated. "I don't know the answer to that one. Keep your wits about you."

CHAPTER 24

I managed a snack and hydrated before Kevin called to ask if I was ready. We agreed on a meeting place. I texted Wade with the information before I left. Kevin was already at the park waiting when I got there.

"How are you? Ready for a run?"

I laughed. "You can probably run circles around me. For you, it will likely be more of a fast walk or jog."

"Don't worry about it. It's cooling off nicely. I can do walking, enjoying the scenery and the company. It's hard to talk while running anyway. Over-rated."

"Okay, well, let's go. Did you have a destination in mind?" The park had a number of different trails that all circled around and intersected each other. Once, I'd gotten confused and another runner on the trail pointed out if you stay to the left you'll get back to where you started. If you go to the right and then left, you'll come out at a different point. I never tested his theory, but left had gotten me out.

"Doesn't matter to me. Water? Car locked? Let's go."

I nodded to each question and he made for the closest trail to where we parked. Pocketing my phone and keys, I joined him.

"Stacie, about all I know about you is that you were married to Theodore Noth, suspected of his murder, and named by him to be on the board of the foundation he funded in death. Oh, and you are very cautious, do yoga, and have a Maltese who warns you when you're in danger. What about family? Career?"

I laughed. "I'm the oldest in my family, the first and only to attend college. One brother. Originally from New York. My brother is career army so I don't see him much. My mother passed away – cancer – some years ago. My father manages a construction company in New York and New Jersey." I smiled. "He spends most of his time upstate these days. He's getting married in a couple of months."

"From your smile, I guess you're okay with that?"

"I am. She's a nice lady and he's happy."

"I know you work. What do you do?"

"I work in HR at Foster's Insurance Group. It's a combination of taking care of all the personnel and benefits stuff and providing employee assistance services as needed. I get to use my social work training and my accounting skills all at once."

"Which do you enjoy more?"

"The accounting part is structured and predictable. Numbers don't lie and I can work a spreadsheet to generate reports in my sleep. The employee assistance part is my adrenalin fix – my opportunity to feel like I can do something to help someone else. It's a good balance for me. Your turn, tell me about your basketball career."

"I made it to the pros, but always second string. What I have going for me is that I'm dependable. My stats are steady, my game doesn't run hot and cold. But I'm no star. I'm the guy they want on the bench when a star needs a rest or is injured. And that's worked out for me."

"You've mentioned experience with domestic violence..."

He exhaled. "My sister, Krystle, used to be married. When she landed in the hospital on one of my infrequent visits home, it was obvious to me what was going on. She stayed because she didn't have enough money and didn't want to be a burden on the rest of the family. My niece suffered from the situation as well. Thanks to basketball I was able to fix that, and help my parents and siblings, but I'm basically a middle class guy. I guess that wasn't in whatever information you and Stewart reviewed?"

"Nope. We really weren't given much information. I remember you come from a small town and large family, played sports in high school then college and then pro." I stopped and turned to face him. "It seemed like some years were missing."

He chuckled. "Four years in the army between high school and college. What college I had, was paid for by Uncle Sam. You could have asked, you know."

I shrugged. "Seemed invasive, maybe none of my business."

"Okay. Can I ask you a question that may be invasive and none of my business?"

"You can ask and then I'll decide if I want to answer."

He nodded, "Fair enough. How is that you are so cautious? I'm not knocking it by the way."

"Not sure it was any one thing. Training in trauma services. Working with victims. A few close calls with dates in college, knowing others who weren't so lucky. Taking self-defense. Talking to women about ways to be safe."

He went to open his mouth and the sound of pounding feet made us both stop. He pulled me over to the side as it got louder. One man and then more behind him came toward us. All in camo and I couldn't help but smile as I spotted Wade in the pack. I felt Kevin tense up and touched his arm.

"It's okay. I know one of them. No offense, but one of those safety rules? Always tell someone where you will be."

The first two men passed and Wade stepped out. I smiled. "Kevin McNair meet Wade Fleetwood. He works for a private security company."

The two men stared at each other until Kevin broke the stand-off.

"Nice to meet you and glad to know someone has Stacie's back." He extended his hand and Wade responded in kind.

"Pleasure to meet you Kevin. I've watched you play. Maybe we could do some one-on-one hoops sometime."

"Always up for anything related to basketball."

"My men are way ahead of me. Enjoy your 'run' and, Stacie, be sure to call Jillie when you get home."

With that, Wade turned and ran in the direction of the other men.

"Who is Jillie?"

"Jillian is his wife and my best friend. They're coming over to watch the interview with us on Thursday. Wade agrees with you on the outcome."

"Any other reasons for being so suspicious?"

I took a deep breath and told him the painful truth. "Ted. He cheated on me. He hid things from me. The many people I met through him and his family who were anything but genuine. Hard to know who to trust." As I'd answered. I saw his eyes get dark and his jaw set and then back to his eyes as pools of blue and his jaw relaxed.

"I'm sorry you had to deal with that. Hopefully, you'll be able to get past it."

"I'm glad we had a chance to talk and about something besides the foundation, Kevin."

"Me, too. It's getting dark faster than I expected though. How about an easy jog back to the parking lot?"
The jog was good and helped to diffuse the tension. We confirmed Thursday night and went our separate ways.

CHAPTER 25

I met Smythe in the parking garage and we went up to Langford's office. Never having been to his office, only the conference room, I'd expected it to be buzzing. It was eerily quiet instead. A trio of young people walked around, two males and one female. Must be the staffers. Smythe approached the reception desk.

"Lionel Smythe and Stacie Maroni. We have an appointment with the senator."

"Of course. Have a seat and I'll let him know you're here."

She stood up and disappeared through a door. A few minutes later, she returned, her smile forced and tight. "He'll be right with you."

We waited and I huffed. Never impressed with the belief that making someone wait spoke to one's importance, I turned to Smythe.

"I wrote up some questions. Here, why don't you look them over while we wait." I handed him a copy of the questions I'd typed up. "And, if you're planning on watching the live broadcast, I'm having some people over. Would you like to join us?"

"Thank you, Stacie. That would be better than watching it alone, I think." He finished reading the list of questions and handed me the paper. "These are good. Should give him a hint of what is to come tomorrow."

"Any updates on the incorporation and bylaws?"

"Mr. Trichter and I have been in contact regularly and with all the irregularities, he is loath to move forward."

Senator Langford joined us then and invited us to his office. The office was well appointed with framed documents and portraits attesting to his position as senator. He took his seat behind a mammoth desk and waved to two chairs in front of the desk. We sat down and I realized his office was staged to emphasize his position of power.

"Isn't it great that Barbie wants this interview? It will be good publicity for the foundation, make up for whatever it was that McNair said. Soon we can start on the mission of the foundation and get services and research going."

Smythe cleared his throat. "Senator, we're here because Ms. Blake has a reputation and we want to help make sure that this does, in fact, yield positive effects for the foundation and you personally."

Langford waved his hands around. "No problem. I meet with people all the time. This isn't my first interview, you know." He leaned back and chuckled.

"Sir, will you humor me? I studied her interview approach and Stacie and I came up with questions we think she may ask. It will only take about fifteen minutes I think."

"Okay, Smythe, we can play your game if it makes you feel better. But I am on a tight schedule. So only five questions, you hear."

I glanced down at my questions – ordered in order of how supportive to confrontive they were. Every third question would cover the range.

"If you're in a hurry, perhaps we should get started. The first question has to do with your alliance to the NFL and their domestic violence awareness program. What prompted you to move in that direction?"

Langford leaned forward and his face lit up. "Every day, our citizens are witnessing or being the victims of domestic violence. The video clip that was all over the media a few years back of the football player assaulting a woman in the elevator brought the problem to the public's attention. As a senator and voice of the people I serve here in Virginia, I felt it was my responsibility to generate legislation to better address the problem and formed the alliance with the NFL as they sought to address the problem as well."

He leaned back, quite smug. I asked one more question that I was sure he had been asked before. Again, he came up with a political spin and smiled as if he was truly on camera.

"Thank you, Senator. Can you explain how you became the Chair of the Theodore Noth Foundation, its mission, and the progress thus far."

"Ted was a passionate and wonderful man. He shared my concern for the level of domestic violence and set aside funds to establish a foundation to provide services to the victims of violence, as well as research to try to prevent violence. When he passed away, the general goals of the foundation were articulated as part of his will along with the stipulation that I be appointed as Chair of the foundation. We are making good progress in establishing the board and seeking incorporation as a non-profit. We will begin making grants to address the goals of the foundation in the near future."

Not as practiced, and if Blake did her research, she would attack the accuracy. Limited to two more questions, I decided to go for the most likely given my own conversation with Blake.

"Senator, I understand that the first meeting of the Board was cancelled when the administrative assistant was murdered, the second meeting ended with a shooting in your parking garage, and the third meeting coincided with a fire at the hotel. Can you comment on these incidents please?"

I barely finished reading and Langford lurched forward, face red, and roaring. "How dare you speak to me like that? Who do you think you are? You are simply pawns and you have no clue who you are dealing with. Get out of here. Now. Before I call security."

Already standing, I grabbed Smythe's arm. He resisted. "Senator, Ms. Blake is liable to ask that question. You need to be prepared to answer it."

As the senator moved in our direction, I succeeded in pulling Smythe out of the room and moved quickly to the elevator.

"A disaster. It will be a disaster." Smythe repeated this over and over.

"Mr. Smythe, did you see how angry he got? If that desk wasn't so big, he'd have been in my face."

Smythe shook his head. He'd delayed us enough that the parking garage was emptying out and we didn't stop to chat.

CHAPTER 26

At home, I curled up with Jasper. I kept replaying the senator's tirade and pure, untethered anger. He was a dangerous man, possibly physically as well as politically. I fixed dinner and sat down to read a mystery and try to escape from reality for a while. I was interrupted when my notifications went off and alerted me someone was in my driveway. I watched as O'Hare walked up to the house and looked around before he approached the door. I was on my feet, disarmed the alarm, and opened the door before he rang the bell.

"Detective?"

"Camera's working, I guess. May I come in?"

"Sure. Come on in and have a seat. What's the occasion?" I was guessing from his stiff posture that this was business not social.

"I got a message from Reston PD. Do you know a Lionel Smythe?"

My mouth dropped. "What happened to Mr. Smythe? Please tell me he's okay."

O'Hare nodded. "He's okay. Someone tried to run him off the road and succeeded. He's in the hospital with some bruises, especially from the airbag. He told the officers that he was concerned about your safety, that the two of you had come from a meeting with Senator Langford. He mentioned a shooting in the garage another time the two of you left a meeting there. What can you tell me about the meeting, Stacie?"

"We went there… Let me start at the beginning – well, the middle really. Langford agreed to be on Barbie Blake's talk show tomorrow night."

He rolled his eyes and let out an expletive. "Is he nuts?"

I shrugged. "That is up in the air. Any way, we went there to 'practice' and he assured us he needed no help on interviews. He did agree to humor us, but limited us to five questions. The first three, no issues, though if Barbie's on top of things, she'll catch him on some inaccuracies. The fourth question was one she is likely to ask him and he lost it."

"What was that?"

"She called me and asked me to come on the show. Don't worry, I'm not that stupid. But she mentioned the fire at the Hilton. So, in the role of Blake, I asked him to explain the murder in his elevator, the shooting in the parking lot, and the fire. He went ballistic and if his desk wasn't so big and between us and him, I'm not sure what would have happened. He was livid."

I'd started shaking as I replayed it in my head and finally voiced the threat I'd felt. I took a deep breath and tried to center myself.

"Mr. Smythe tried to explain that Blake was liable to ask the same question and he came at us, and we left – in a hurry. Did Mr. Smythe give them a description of the car?"

"Black compact car. He didn't get a plate number and he didn't see who was driving. He said it happened too fast. If it was Langford, he may have thought you were both in his car."

It wasn't a question but his expression and tilt of his head said otherwise. I laughed.

"We drove separately. Our only connection is the foundation. He's the legal counsel, my dad's age, and in all honesty, he's been a thorn in Langford's side, paying attention to all the details and inconsistencies."

"I know in the past this hasn't worked – is there some place you can stay tonight?"

"Detective, I have a state-of-the-art alarm system, cameras on all sides, a nosy neighbor who calls the police frequently, and my ferocious dog. I'll be fine."

He stood up. "That's what I thought. I'll ask for additional coverage in the neighborhood. You hear anything or Jasper acts funny, you call. Then again, it may have nothing to do with your meeting."

My phone rang and I put up my hand as I read the callerID.

"Senator Langford?"

"Hello, Stacie. I wanted to call and apologize for my behavior this afternoon. It has been a long day. I understand that you and Smythe were only doing what you felt was needed. Perhaps the two of us could meet to review those questions?"

"I'm sorry, sir, I have company right now and he's not leaving for some time. And, of course, I work all day tomorrow. I could email you the list of questions we'd come up with though."

"That's not necessary. Everything will be fine."

"Thank you for calling, Senator."

I hung up. O'Hare waited.

"He apologized for his outburst and asked me to meet with him – the two of us. Ostensibly to finish going through the questions. Only then he said he didn't want the questions, so I don't believe him."

"Neither do I. You got any coffee? If so, I may hang around a while just in case."

I nodded and went into the kitchen. As I came back with his coffee, I caught the end of his conversation.

"… in about twenty you think? See you then."

"You'll barely have time to drink your coffee if you have to be somewhere in twenty minutes."

"I'm going to sit right here, unless a call comes in. Napoli is off duty and she's going to come by and leave her car in your driveway for the night. I'll drive her home and she'll have Reardon bring her by in the morning to get her car."

I smiled as I figured out the ploy. It would look like someone was here with me all night.

"Detective, is this level of interest and assistance typical of Beckman PD?"

He smiled. "No. Not at all. Somehow from the start, you were different from most of our suspects or victims. You don't go out of your way to get in trouble – it just finds you. Definitely different, and I do mean that in a good way."

Not quite sure how to take that, I was saved from having to respond by the notification that someone was in my driveway. I walked outside with O'Hare to say hello to Marina. Nope, most people weren't on a first name basis with police officers or detectives. I thanked them both and holed up in my house with my fancy alarm system and ferocious dog.

CHAPTER 27

Sleep didn't come easy. I tried some yoga positions and even dragged the counter island to block the kitchen door just in case. With alarm and camera notifications turned on, I had to focus on not ignoring them or discounting the alert as the wind or a bird. It was stimulus overload and the temptation was there though, especially with Jasper fast asleep.

I finally got up, moved the island out of the way, disarmed the alarm and let Jasper out. Once he was back inside, I reset the alarm and finished my coffee. Marina's car was still in the driveway and all was quiet. Almost ready to leave for work, I was cleaning up when a car pulled in. Marina and Reardon both got out. I joined them outside, ready to leave for work.

"Good morning. It looks like a great day."

"Morning yourself and thanks for leaving your car here. Not sure it was necessary…"

While Marina and I exchanged pleasantries, Reardon walked around my car and then Marina's.

"I don't see any evidence of anyone tampering. No problems last night?"

"No, it was pretty uneventful. I could live with that for a while."

He smiled. "Okay, we'll be on our way. Stay safe, Stacie."

"Thanks, and same to you guys."

After the stress of the evening before, it seemed a little anticlimactic to go to work. I wondered at what the day would bring. I'd emailed Smythe to see how he was doing. So far, he hadn't responded.

Work held no surprises. At lunch, I shared the incident with Langford and Smythe's accident with my friends. We all agreed the interview would be a disaster or worse. Jillian and Wade were already coming to watch the show and I extended the invitation to Ronnie and Trina.

After lunch, I had some time and on a whim decided to call Meredith Langford. I hadn't talked to her since Ted's murder. She'd told me what the senator had told her not to tell the police. I dialed and was surprised when she answered.

"Hello?"

"Hi Meredith. This is Stacie Maroni. Sorry to bother you. Working with your father on Ted's foundation, I was thinking of you. How are you doing these days?"

She hesitated before she responded. "This is a surprise. I'm... I'm doing okay. Keeping busy. Some volunteer work, you know the routine."

"Good. I'm glad to hear it. Hopefully, no more run ins with the person who assaulted you. Are you seeing anyone these days?"

She chuckled. "As you can imagine, that is what my parents want, especially my mother. She drags me places with hopes of introducing me. Makes me glad I'm out of circulation for a while."

"Oh?"

"Yeah, I was in a car wreck a week ago – totaled my car and ended up with whiplash and some other injuries."

"That's terrible. How'd it happen?"

"We think it was just a freak accident. Remember the day it rained so bad? I was driving in the worst of it, I braked, and the car spun out of control."

"That must have been scary. I'm glad you're okay though."

"Thanks, and thanks for calling, Stacie."

She disconnected. I couldn't help but wonder if someone had tampered with her brakes. Unfortunately, she hadn't volunteered any information about the senator. I thought about all I knew and the most puzzling piece was the inclusion of Bryce on the board. Why would Langford invite someone he systematically voted at odds with? It made no sense to me. Maybe Blake would ask him about that or his sudden change in voting pattern. I tried to call Smythe again, with no luck.

CHAPTER 28

I left work early and stopped to pick up some beer, wine and cheese. And Rocky Road ice cream – after all, it was on sale. Jillian and Wade arrived, and then Kevin. Trina and Ronnie had other plans. I had the television set for the Barbie Blake Show and barely had time to get everyone a drink. I noticed Wade and Kevin over near the door in discussion and looked to Jillian for an explanation. She shrugged.

I put down the drinks and they joined us. Then I pulled out my sheet of questions to see how close Smythe and I had guessed at her approach. Kevin studied them and winced at one, but I didn't get a chance to ask which one.

The first few were close if not exactly what we'd guessed. Blake asked him about his successes, with pretend innocence.

As he visibly relaxed, she brought up the foundation and his position on domestic violence. He kept his answer short and vague, a smile on his face as he discussed the problems with violence. Her next question on the board members had his smile waning. He explained the vetting process – not the initial one, but the final one – and even mentioned Smythe as overseeing it.

Blake seemed taken back by his answer with a slight frown before she bubbled up again. "Senator Langford, I understand Senator Bryce is also involved in the foundation." At his nod and tight smile, she commented, "Didn't the two of you face off on the gambling legislation in the past?"

Langford twitched slightly before he answered. "There are always two sides to a coin and Clarisse and I differed in opinion on gambling. We're both on the same side when it comes to violence though." His smug smile was the tell he thought he'd skated by that one.

With a change in her body tilt and set of mouth, Wade commented, "She's about to go for his jugular or at least she thinks she is."

"Senator, I understand you've had three meetings of members of the board and only with the last one established who was on the board. Is that correct?"

Kevin interjected, "She's leading him down the primrose path."

Langford responded, "That's correct. The members of the board were formally identified after the vetting process at the last meeting."

"And that last meeting was at the Hilton, correct? The same night as a fire?"

"I do recall a fire alarm disrupting the meeting; however, it was on the other side of the hotel." He smiled, smug.

"And the shooting in the parking lot after the second meeting? Or the murder of your administrative assistant before the first meeting?"

"Ms. Blake, both of those are being investigated by the appropriate authorities. I'm sure they will come up with a reasonable explanation." His tone reflected tension, but he still had a smile on his face.

"Interesting. Do you believe in coincidence, Senator?"

He hesitated. "I've never given it any thought. If I'm on a highway and there's an accident – that's a coincidence if I'm not directly involved, same as anyone else on the same highway. I guess I do believe there are coincidences." He smiled, pleased with his answer.

"Is it a coincidence then that the members of the board are the same ones suggested by some unidentified person? Or that you neglected to include Stacie Maroni on many of your emails regarding foundation business? Or that the young man…"

"I don't know where you got your information. I don't have to deal with this." His face was purple and he stood up. We all leaned forward and the station immediately cut to commercial.

"Stacie, is that what happened last night? That raw rage?" Wade looked concerned.

I nodded. Kevin turned to me, questions in his expression. I provided a brief recap before the station returned to the interview. Amazingly to me, Langford was seated and calm. Blake looked a little more tentative.

"Senator, I invited Kevin McNair and Stacie Maroni to join us. They both declined. Do you have any idea why?"

"Obviously they do not have the same level of commitment to making Ted's dream come true. Why else?" He preened and added, "I've already suggested to Ms. Maroni that it might be a good idea for her to separate herself from the foundation, as has Ted's father. As for Mr. McNair, I believe even you questioned his motives."

"Back to the negative occurrences, I understand legal counsel for the foundation was in a car accident after he left a meeting with you last night. Is the crime level that high in the area of the Langford building?"

Langford blanched and quickly recovered. "I was not aware of that. I hope Mr. Smythe was not injured. As you know crime rates have increased considerably over time nationally and Reston is not without its fair share. You mentioned the gambling legislation and one of the reasons I objected to legalizing gambling has to do with the kinds of seedy individuals, loan sharks, and crime that often move in when gambling becomes more rampant. That said, I have faith the authorities will find the responsible individuals in due time."

"Canned speech if I ever heard one." Kevin commented before Blake could respond.

"One more question, Senator, how is it working with Senator Bryce on the board? I understand the two of you don't see eye-to-eye on many issues, including gambling."

Langford paled and his hands gripped the arms of his chair. "The board is coming together and we will get to foundation business in the near future."

I expected Blake to attack again. Instead, she looked to the side and with a slight nod directed her attention back to Langford.

"Senator, thank you for coming in today."

"Thank you for having me."

"Did you catch that? Someone prompted her to end it. What's that all about? Kevin, how did that work when you were on the show?"

"Honestly? I was so blindsided with her questions I'm not sure of the events at the end. In the prep part, Barbie and her boss explained the prompters who would let her know when it was time to cut to commercial or time was running out. With me, she tried to get me back on after the commercial like she did there with Langford. I told her I was done and left – her boss didn't look too thrilled."

Wade sneered. "I watched that interview to the end. She seemed uncomfortable finishing up without someone to banter with even for a few minutes. Here? I'm guessing her boss figured they'd gotten whatever rise from him they'd get. During the commercial someone must have but a bug in his ear – I mean literally. I'm betting someone did damage control and prompted him to talk about general crime and not take her bait."

"But did you notice how he reacted to the mere mention of Bryce? That wasn't anger, it was pure fear."

Everyone nodded.

The debacle of the interview talked out, a sudden, almost awkward, silence enveloped the room. I jumped up with the pretense of getting more drinks and asked if anyone was hungry. Cheese and crackers only went so far.

When I returned, the tension between Wade and Kevin was palpable, with Jillian's eyes wide as the two men stared at each other.

"Simple question, McNair. Why carry when you come to Stacie's house? Even if you have a permit and it's legal. Most of us don't carry on a date or at a social event."

"I have a permit. It is legal. And I always carry. So far, at least twice with Stacie, it's been to both our advantages."

"That doesn't answer the question. Most basketball players don't carry. What are you hiding?"

Kevin took a deep breath and glanced at the three of us.

"I'll have that beer you're holding, Stacie. It's a long story. When I graduated from high school, there weren't many options. I wasn't able to land an athletic scholarship, so I worked security for a while. That didn't pay so great and I enlisted, ended up in the MPs – military police. I still dreamed of playing basketball and so I played every chance I got. I was young back then."

He took a slug from the bottle and then he continued. "I did my four years, got the GI bill, played in college, and went pro. By then I went pro for the money, not the fame. I'd outgrown the dream. Being a professional athlete pays well even when you're not the star, and my sister was able to get out of an abusive relationship and pursue her own dreams. I also helped out my brothers and parents."

"And your dreams?"

"Me? I'm tired of travelling eight months a year and maybe even playing overseas in the summer. I'm not in any hurry, but I'm no spring chicken and I'd like to settle down. My agent isn't happy, but I won't be playing basketball professionally next season."

"So, what will you do?"

He smiled and winked at me. "I applied and was accepted into the police academy with the Reston PD. The interview was the appointment I was leaving when I bumped into you that day outside the Yoga Pod."

He shrugged at my open mouth. "I didn't know Chief Rizzo was on the board and he didn't know I'd expressed an interest in the foundation until that meeting at the Langford Building. That's what we were talking about after the meeting that night."

He turned to Wade, "I guess the answer to your question is I'm a basketball player with a policing background and future, and yes, I carry pretty much all the time except at sports events or other venues where it's not legal."

Any further conversation was derailed by the doorbell. I glanced at the camera feed. "It's Rick?"

I went to the door to see what he wanted. "Hi. Come on in."

"Your driveway looks like there's a party going on." He nodded to each of them and only registered surprise on seeing Kevin. Jasper immediately went to him and he picked him up. My computer started to ping and he put up his hand.

"Flatt is checking the perimeter."

Both Wade and Kevin stood up and there was a knock on the door.

"You can relax. That's Flatt."

Wade went to let him in and Rick waited to get the all clear from Flatt. "Did you happen to catch the Barbie Blake Show tonight?"

We all nodded. Flatt shifted his weight from one foot to the other.

"O'Hare wanted to make sure you were safe – keep that alarm system armed. If needed, we can arrange for someone to park their car in your drive again for the next couple nights. Let O'Hare know."

"Thank you both. I appreciate the extra attention."

Flatt nodded and after a pause stated, "Come on. We got a call. Later, Stacie and all."

CHAPTER 29

"Did something happen other than Langford losing his cool last night?"

Wade and Jillian nodded to Kevin's question. I was spared answering the question by another alert. The car in the live feed wasn't familiar, but I recognized the person getting out of it.

"Leaving the meeting, Smythe was run off the road. That's him."

Both Wade and Kevin followed me as I opened the door. "Mr. Smythe, come on in. I heard about your accident. Are you okay?" His face was bruised and he was missing his usual bowtie.

"I am Stacie. Hello, Kevin." Smythe looked at Wade as Jillian joined us.

"Forgive me. Introductions first. Wade and Jillian Fleetwood – Lionel Smythe. Wade and Jillian are my good friends, Mr. Smythe is legal counsel for the foundation. Why don't we all sit down. Somebody want to order a pizza or something? I'll grab a couple more beers." I escaped into the kitchen returning with beers and bottled water.

Wade was on the phone and disconnected. "Pizza's ordered. About 30 minutes. You were about to tell us about Mr. Smythe's accident. Mr. Smythe, can you tell us what happened?"

"Please, please call me Lionel. We had just left the meeting with Langford and he was very angry with us. I was trying to think out how or why this usually controlled man had lost it. What about the question Stacie asked triggered such an emotional reaction. So I wasn't paying much attention other than to speed and lights. All of a sudden, a black compact car reamed into the side of my car. I registered the car moving into my lane and the next thing I knew I was on a stretcher. I told the police and paramedics and asked them to notify someone in Beckman Springs to be sure you were safe. Did they contact you, Stacie?"

"Yes, and thank you. Detective O'Hare stopped by to let me know. Then the senator called to apologize and asked me to meet with him. I told him I had company and didn't expect my company to leave for a while." I turned my attention to Kevin, Wade, and Jillian. "O'Hare arranged for Marina – Officer Napoli – to leave her car in the drive all night. Her partner brought her by this morning to pick it up."

"Good, good. I'm sorry I didn't make your interview party. I only caught bits and pieces from the police station."

"What happened now?"

He exhaled. "A good stiff drink is in order, but I'll have one of those waters, Stacie. I spent the last few hours with Chief Rizzo. He initially tried to tell me it was my pain meds talking, but I didn't give up. I think Bryce is the problem, not Langford."

Wade perked up. "Or both of them. I haven't had a chance to share what I found out with Stacie or verify it. It looks like Bryce is a silent partner in at least one of the major casinos coming into Virginia for starters."

Smythe nodded and sneered. "I chose to specialize in trusts and non-profits to avoid all the conflict and chicanery of criminal law. Everyone involved has to declare any conflicts of interest, financial or legal. When a quick background check yields some irregularities, a quick phone call usually straightens it out, no problem. To cut to the chase, shortly before our meeting with Senator Langford, I called Senator Bryce about some companies I never heard of and couldn't easily determine if they would bias her decision-making."

He paused and, curious, I asked. "Like what? I mean couldn't all of our jobs bias our decision-making?"

"Yes, but we all know you work at Cornerstone and are Mr. Noth's widow. If Cornerstone wanted to put in a grant application, you and Shawna would have to recuse yourselves and not be part of the discussion. Awkward, yes. Same with Mr. Beasley if someone wants to do research on aggression and domestic violence in the NFL. He would not be part of it, and likely we would ask Mr. McNair here to recuse himself as well. It's the hidden things that can be problematic."

Wade nodded. "Other than what I mentioned, what else did you find?"

"The silent partner is 'silent' because it is through one of many corporations – including Rusticroad. Stacie, that has a web address, but when you go to the next layer, it's under another corporation. Each of the ones the background check pulled was in fact a 'dummy' under another corporation."

"Wait! The grant that was supposedly awarded? Wasn't that the [dot] com email address?"

"Yes. I asked her to provide me with information to determine if there was a conflict so that when the board actually sees the proposal, she is not part of the discussion or decision. She became quite upset and threatening, much as Langford was at our meeting. Accused me of violation of privacy and stalking and racism. She signed, as did you all, consent to the background check. She made a few comments about her power and told me to be careful who I pushed. Quite intimidating. Unfortunately for me, I advised her I had a meeting with Senator Langford and we'd have to finish our conversation another day."

"Given my accident, and that I was only about two blocks from the Langford Building, Chief Rizzo had already checked the outside video streams. The senator hadn't left the building when I was run off the road."

He added, "Yes, he could have arranged it – called his go-to person for shooting or breaking and entering if we think he's responsible for all these incidents – but I was only two blocks from the building. It's more likely someone knew I was there and was waiting for me to leave."

I sat back.

"What happens next?" Kevin was the first to ask the obvious question.

"With all the 'coincidences' and the emails with some of the [dot] coms matching Bryce's dummy companies, Chief Rizzo and I met with the District Attorney. They were on their way over to Senator Bryce's home and I came here. There were police officers waiting for Senator Langford when he finished his interview with Blake. He was allowed to go home once the video stream cleared him rather than wait for his attorney to show up. Where is the pizza? I'm hungry."

As if on cue, the pizza delivery arrived and we all stopped talking long enough to enjoy our pizza. We rehashed Langford's interviews, each of us picking apart one of his statements. Silence was immediate when Smythe's phone rang.

"Hello."

"Yes, Chief, I understand."

"Right now I'm at Stacie Maroni's home in Beckman Springs."

"Thank you."

He hung up and shook his head. "Senator Bryce wouldn't speak with the DA or the Chief without her attorney present. With both Senators on alert to potential arrest, they're requesting that Beckman Springs PD come here and follow me to Reston. I'll be spending the night in some place unknown until further notice."

My mouth dropped. "Wow."

Kevin cleared his throat. "Stacie, he's not the only one at risk or a potential target from one or both senators."

Before I could respond, more company arrived. I recognized O'Hare's car and the police car was easily identified. I let O'Hare, Flatt, and Rick in. Their grim expressions reflected a whole new level of seriousness.

"Mr. Smythe?"

"Lionel Smythe, meet some of Beckman Springs' finest. From what Chief Rizzo told you, I guess they're your police escort?"

O'Hare shook hands with Smythe. "Mr. Smythe, Officers Flatt and Murdock will follow you to the meet in Reston. Stay safe."

Smythe moved slowly, still holding his plate.

"Wait, can I wrap that up for you?" To O'Hare, I added, "Is that okay?"

Both nodded and I dashed into the kitchen for a baggie and shoved his pizza inside. I gave him a hug as he left with Flatt and Murdock.

O'Hare made no move to leave. He stared at me while everyone else remained silent.

To break the ice, I asked, "Have you met Kevin McNair? Want some pizza?"

He glared for a second, then shifted his attention to my friends and nodded to Kevin. "I gather you all know what's happening in Reston and the potential fall-out? We will step up our watch in this neighborhood. The reality is if there's a call, though, the car assigned will respond to the call. Any suggestions?"

I noticed he looked to Wade and Kevin, not Jillian or me, and I bristled. "I do have this amazing alarm system, video surveillance, and a ferocious dog."

"And if whoever were to come here had an accomplice create mayhem somewhere else to divert my officers, they could cut your electricity and your alarm system would be useless. Yes, we'd get a call that your alarm system was out. And our response time could be longer than ideal while you sit here in the dark." O'Hare's speech was clipped and crisp.

"If it's all right with Stacie, I can stay here. I have experience and I'm armed." Kevin reached for his wallet as he started to speak and handed his permit to O'Hare.

O'Hare glanced at it and handed it back. "Is that agreeable to everyone else?"

"Stacie?" Kevin asked.

"That'll work. Wait, what about Shaq?"

"I'll call my sister and see if she can check on him tonight and in the morning."

O'Hare nodded and stood up. "Anything changes, anything happens, don't hesitate to call."

Wade and Kevin walked O'Hare to the door. I turned to Jillian and threw my hands up in the air. She grinned and teased, "Don't you usually go out on a date before a guy spends the night?"

I fake punched her. "Shush! When did my life get so crazy?"

Wade and Kevin came back and joined us. We all chatted for a while and cleaned up the mess. At Wade's insistence, I let Jasper out and back in before he and Jillian took off.

CHAPTER 30

After the first awkward moments of Kevin and me, alone in my townhouse, we both started to speak at the same time.

"I can just…"

"Can I get…"

Then in unison, "You first." We both started laughing. He recovered first.

"This will be fine. I just need a pillow and blanket if you've got them handy and I'll sleep right here on the couch. There's no other way in besides the front door and the kitchen door, right?"

"No other doors, no. There is a guest room, but it's… I wasn't expecting company."

"The best place for me is between entry and you. The couch is fine. I've slept on worse."

"But it's too short."

"Stacie, it's fine. The most important thing right now is your safety. Now, where is your ferocious dog?" He chuckled and on cue, Jasper showed up at his feet. "Come on, Jasper, you and I need to strategize."

Jasper tilted his head and then lay down. We both laughed.

"Seriously, walk me through your alarm system and how the cameras are set up."

I nodded and brought my laptop over to the computer. I reviewed the system with him and he let Jasper out again to see the camera notification. As expected, the area lit up with Jasper's movement. It was getting late and we checked all the doors and windows.

"If it's okay with you, I'm going to get my gym bag out of my car and change into shorts and a tee shirt."

"Yeah, sure. Let me get you a blanket and pillow. I'll be right back."

I grabbed those things and my "treat bag" from the dentist. At least he could brush his teeth. He came in with his bag and took the stuff from me.

"I'm going to turn in and you should do the same. You have to work tomorrow, right?"

I nodded. "Okay. Good night. Help yourself to anything you need."

Expecting to see Jasper behind me, I shook my head as he curled up on the pillow for Kevin. He shrugged. "We'll work it out. Good night."

My phone beeped and I heard Jasper barking and howling. I jumped up and ran into the living area. Kevin was on the floor with the laptop in the dark except for a small night light.

"Call 9-1-1. No light. You have company. Two individuals, male. I'm assuming uninvited."

I dialed 9-1-1. "Yes, emergency. This is Stacie Maroni. Two men are trying to break into my house. Let Detective O'Hare know, please."

"You're on the blotter. We'll send someone out. Hold on."

"Thank you."

My phone rang and I jumped. Rick. "Hi, Rick."

"What can you tell me? Is anyone there with you?"

"Yes, Kevin. I'm handing him the phone." He took the phone and pulled me down to the floor beside him. He spoke softly into the phone, not quite a whisper, but not a normal volume either.

"Hey, Murdock. Two men. One keeps walking around the house – he's checking windows, one outside the kitchen. Their movement triggered a notification, but the lights aren't coming on. Odd. Came on earlier with Jasper. Only light is from street lights."

"Only light inside is night light. We're on the floor in front of the sofa. Screen is away from window."

He laughed quietly. "Yeah, right. What's your ETA?"

"Got it. I'm going to put the phone on speaker but turn the volume down."

He set the phone on the floor after lowering the volume and hit speaker. "Can you hear us?"

I barely heard Rick's response, something about Jasper, who was still growling, but tilted his head at Rick's voice. Kevin whispered to me, "They're approaching on foot. Stay down and keep quiet."

The alarm went off, and Kevin pulled me down to the floor. "Kitchen door contact. Not in yet." He had his gun in his right hand, waiting.

I whispered, "I have to call Reston Security."

Kevin shook his head, "No, this is why you have the system, Stacie."

Another beep. "Murdock, if that's not you, we have a third man." Another beep, from a different camera and another man.

There was action on three cameras and it was hard to decide which one to look at. And with minimal light, it was hard to see much. I was watching the guy in the camera outside the kitchen door as another man came up behind him. It looked like he said something, and the first guy turned. The other one punched him and drew his weapon. I heard Rick whisper, "This one moves and he's dead. Where's his partner?"

"Around the corner. He's managed to disappear a couple times – a blind spot. There's also someone angling in between you and him. Flatt, I hope."

Another beep and someone walking up the sidewalk toward the front step. No light came on though.

"More company, Murdock. He stopped and now is coming in your direction."

"O'Hare. You have eyes on Flatt and the other guy?"

"Only the one I think is Flatt – stocky build. Wait. Everyone is heading in your direction."

We watched the action but couldn't quite tell who was who or what was happening. Then everything stopped.

"Situation neutralized. Can you come open the door back here? And Stacie, now you can call Reston Security."

Rick chortled and Kevin smiled. His eyes twinkled with a spark and he shook his head. He picked up the phone and turned off the speaker, then stood and pulled me up.

In the kitchen, he opened the door slowly and only when he saw Rick, O'Hare, and Flatt with two guys in cuffs did he put his gun away. The group moved through the kitchen and out the front door. Rick trotted off to get their car, parked on another street.

My phone rang and Kevin handed it to me. Reston Security. I verified the problem and that it was under control. Rick pulled up and he and Flatt took the two intruders away. O'Hare assured them he'd be there soon. He came back inside briefly.

"Did you recognize either of them?"

I shook my head.

"Okay, we'll see what we can find out. I'll be in touch. Barricade that back door – second time. And find out why the motion sensors didn't activate the lights. They should have." The last part was directed to Kevin, not me.

After Jasper went out, we locked up, barricaded the kitchen door, and reset all the alarms. It hit me all at once and I started to shake. My efforts to hold it together failed when Kevin pulled me into his arms.

"It's okay. You're safe."

CHAPTER 31

I stumbled into bed and surprised myself by falling asleep. The next I knew, I awoke to the smell of coffee. After a quick face wash and pulling a comb through my hair, I found Kevin staring into my refrigerator, Jasper at his feet. I watched him silently and smiled. A sound made me turn and Wade shrugged as I jumped.

"Good morning, Stacie. Kevin and I have been busy this morning."

"Morning. I called Wade to help figure out why your lights didn't come on last night and why there was a blind spot to camera three."

I breathed a sigh of relief they weren't killing each other. "Did you figure it out?"

Kevin rolled his hand back and forth and smiled. "Not sure. We have a theory. Still working on it, but I needed coffee and some food. Hungry?"

I yawned. "Coffee first, please. Did you find what you were looking for in the fridge?"

He laughed. "You won't starve though you're short on the veggies. I'm guessing you eat a lot of sandwiches."

"Did you check her freezer?" Wade chuckled.

I waited for Kevin's expression when he opened the freezer door. He closed the door and turned around, mouth open and eyes wide.

"It was on sale. I couldn't pass it up."

"I counted six half-gallons of ice cream. Did I count wrong?"

"You missed one then. Probably in the door – I don't think I finished it yet."

"Kevin, I don't know if you noticed, but I'm betting that's not just any ice cream either, but all Rocky Road." Wade winked and laughed at the stunned expression on Kevin's face.

"My addiction and favorite comfort food."

Kevin shook his head and handed me a cup of coffee.

I took a few sips. "Okay, brain is starting to wake up. What's going on?"

Wade nodded to Kevin to respond. "Wade gave me his number last night. I texted to see if he was awake. He called, I filled him in, and here he is. We're going to figure out what happened to your lights and check what looked like a blind spot. We were heading outside when you got up. Sit. Drink your coffee. Hold off on the ice cream until after breakfast?"

I snorted. "Sorry. I will do my best. Take Jasper with you."

I sat down with my coffee and laptop and watched them as they walked the perimeter. Sure enough, for camera number three, they disappeared and then reappeared after a couple of yards. Huh. The door opened and I jumped.

"Only us." Jasper came over and I picked him up.

"Why didn't I just see you? Did you figure it out?"

"We're not sure when they did this, but could probably figure it out if we went through all your video stream for the past few weeks. Two of the bulbs were missing, a third was busted, and the fourth – the one outside this door was the only one projecting any light."

Wade interjected, "But… it had a half cone around it, leaving the area immediately below it in the dark. You wouldn't notice it when you let Jasper out. You'd think it was working."

He looked to Kevin to continue. "There was a cone on number three as well, so no light and blocked access results in a person disappearing into the shadows. They must have figured that would be one you might notice if it didn't light up once in a while. Once they got past the first one, the darkness protected them."

I nodded and exhaled. So much for my state-of-the-art surveillance system. My phone rang, Jillian.

"Hi Jillian. You missing Wade?"

"Yeah, I was kind of surprised when he lit out of here like your house was on fire. Really though, he told me what happened last night. Girl, you need to take a sick day and hunker down."

"I know you're right…"

"Then, what's the problem? You have the best protection in the world – Wade, that is – and dreamy, intense blue eyes. Stay put until this mess is cleaned up."

"Okay. I have to go. I can see Kevin and Wade scheming over here."

Kevin opened the refrigerator door again and closed it. "Anyone up for breakfast tacos?"

I stared at him. "Uh, I doubt you found the makings for tacos in my fridge."

"Nope. I'm going to go get some. What's your preference?"

In a few minutes with some quibbling over who would pay, Kevin left. I fed Jasper and waited to hear Wade's words of wisdom.

"You want my opinion?"

"You're going to give it anyway, aren't you?"

"Of course." He snickered. "He is way too smooth, too good to be true. On the other hand, there is a consistency and the no nonsense attitude. I'll give him the benefit of the doubt unless you tell me he was a jerk last night."

I smiled. "Nope. Perfect gentleman. We talked for a while and then went to sleep until the cameras detected movement and I got up. Afterward, I think we were both too tired to even talk. I'm not sure he actually went to sleep though."

Wade nodded. As the laptop pinged, we both watched as Kevin's car pulled in the driveway. Wade went to let him in as my phone rang.

"Hi Dad. What's up?"

"Deanna told me some talk show host mentioned your name. Is this about that foundation again?"

"She interviewed Senator Langford, and yes, they mentioned the foundation."

"I looked him up, Langford. Odd, his wife? I've seen someone who looked a lot like her in Atlantic City. Then again, they say we all have a twin somewhere. I don't know her name, but she made a scene in the casino and had to be helped to leave by security. Drunk and not particularly lucky from what I heard."

"Probably someone else."

Wade and Kevin walked back in bantering and joking.

"You have company?"

"Wade and Kevin are here. We're having coffee and hopefully some breakfast."

"Kevin who and why are they there so early?"

I could hear the edge in my father's voice. "Someone tried to break in last night and they've been trying to figure out why the motion detectors didn't light up the whole neighborhood. They figured it out and worked up an appetite in the process."

"Did they get whoever it was?"

"Yes, they did. Two men. They were taken into custody last night."

"Now, who is this Kevin person and how is he involved in all this?"

"Kevin is …" Kevin stopped talking mid-sentence and stared at me. Wade started laughing.

"Kevin is about my age, a veteran, and an athlete. He has a security background from the army. He's also on the board and somehow this all seems connected."

Kevin tilted his head and smiled. I almost burst out laughing. On the side, Wade was mouthing, "You're in trouble now."

"And he just happens to be there?"

"Yes, Dad. He brought breakfast tacos and they're getting cold."

"Okay, Stacie, but be careful. Stay safe and keep me posted on what's happening, you hear? Not just on the foundation but on this Kevin person."

"Will do. You take care and tell Deanna I said hi."

I disconnected and put my head in my hands, embarrassed.

"I only heard your side of the conversation obviously. Does your dad always grill you about who's in your house?"

"Only males. He knows Wade and Jillian, so he doesn't count."

Wade chuckled. "He's the one who put all the cameras in and arranged for the alarm system."

"You said he lives in New York or New Jersey, right? Visit often?"

"Not too often. When he feels like it or Nate, my attorney and family friend, lets him know something's happening. Then he just shows up. Maybe that will stop when he marries Deanna."

The laptop pinged again. A very tired looking O'Hare lumbered up the drive, hopefully with information and good news.

CHAPTER 32

Kevin went to get the door while Wade shook his head, grinning from ear to ear. I shook my head at him and cleaned up our taco mess.

"Come in, have a seat. Can I get you a cup of coffee, Detective?"

He nodded and collapsed into the seat. Another person who hadn't been to sleep yet. I got the coffee for him and sat down.

"What can you tell us? Who were they? Why were they here? What did they want?"

"Lots of questions there, Stacie. They were a couple of lowlifes for hire. Brothers, both of them have records longer than you are tall. Initially, neither of them was willing to talk. We confiscated their phones and checked the frequently called numbers and received calls. We're following up on those."

Wade coughed. "Any ideas, off the record."

O'Hare shook his head. "Langford is definitely involved, but none of those numbers matched any phones we have on record. On a whim, I threw out Langford's name as they were coming into the station. The older brother has a drug problem and he folded at that. He and his brother were hired to scare you and anyone else 'the boss' felt could jeopardize some business with the foundation. Every time one of them did anything, Langford was notified to let him know they'd hit again."

"Have you talked to Langford yet?"

"The District Attorney was meeting with him and his attorney when I left the station. Langford fell apart. I'm not at liberty to share what he said. Suffice it to say, he is as much the victim here as anyone else. He was being blackmailed and made decisions in many situations based on fear of the secrets being revealed and of others being hurt. Smythe's 'accident' was a little too much for him to handle."

"Anything else you can tell us?"

"Afraid not, Stacie. I will tell you to be very careful – stay home. It probably won't be until later today before it all unfolds. In the meantime, I'm going to go home and crash. Someone, most likely me, will be in touch."

Wade volunteered to hang around so Kevin and I could both take a nap. I woke up several hours later to laughter wafting back to my bedroom. I warred with myself as to whether to shower or go find out what was happening. The shower won and I felt human, though caffeine deprived, as I walked into the living area.

"Dad! What are you doing here?"

"I didn't feel good about our phone call – felt like you were keeping something from me. I was in New Jersey checking on job sites. My foremen are doing their jobs and

I hopped in the car. Three hours later, here I am." He stood and gave me a hug.

"Get yourself a cup of coffee and then you can join Kevin and me. We sent Wade home. He and Jillian will be back later."

I glanced at Kevin, whose expression reminded me of the Cheshire cat with blue eyes. Jasper curled up on the couch next to him. As scary as the thought he and my dad had been talking was, it would be better with coffee. I groaned when I saw the pastry my dad brought. No wonder I wasn't a size six anymore. Plate and coffee in hand, I sat down.

"You feel better, Stacie?"

"Definitely. When did you get here?"

"About an hour ago?" He looked to Kevin for confirmation and Kevin nodded.

"Kevin's been filling me in on all the members of the board. Like I told you, I checked Langford out. I'm sure now the woman I saw in Atlantic City is his wife. Isn't he up for re-election this fall?"

"I think so." I shrugged and looked to Kevin.

"Yes, he is. His platform plays up his easy going, for the people persona, and his work with the NFL and domestic violence. Grass roots activities. He can't afford a scandal right now – whether about his wife, if that is who you saw, Leo, or the foundation. The media seem to think it will be a close race."

"What does all this have to do with me? Or Smythe or Stewart?"

Kevin shrugged. We threw around some more ideas until my stomach growling made a loud retort.

Kevin laughed and my dad shook his head. "Obviously, you cannot survive on a piece of pastry. Your fridge and freezer still look pathetic?"

My mouth dropped and Kevin nodded.

"Let me make a few phone calls and get us some dinner. Maybe Nate will join us." He walked toward the window and made a call.

I looked to Kevin and raised my hands as if to say "What went on?"

With a glance in my dad's direction, he explained, "Your dad wanted to know more about the board and who was on it, why Wade and I were here, and why you weren't at work. Wade and I answered the latter two..." He tilted his hand back and forth to indicate it was a sort of answer they gave my dad.

"Then Wade took off and I was going through the members of the board as best I could. We talked about Beasley. Your dad remembered some plays from one of the Super bowl games. Then we discussed Langford. I was about to move on to Bryce given their animosity toward each other." He shook his head.

My dad joined us. "Dinner and Nate will be here in about 30 minutes. Bryce? Not familiar with him."

"Her. Bryce is a woman. We have women senators, Dad."

"Okay, okay. What do we know about this woman?"

"Politically, she fights racism and racial disparities, all the other isms, and working class. Smythe and Wade found out she's got part interest in the casinos coming into Virginia – the very same ones she just argued and voted for but never mentioned how she'd benefit personally."

"Stacie, that's not too surprising. Politicians are crooked hypocrites – they support laws that benefit themselves and their friends. Doesn't matter what party they're with. She up for re-election, too?"

I shrugged and turned to Kevin. He put up his index finger and then typed on my laptop. "No. She has two more years. According to this site, she's not getting good marks from her constituents. Likely her motivation to be on the board. Still there was a lot of animosity between Langford and Bryce. When they were arguing, he accused her of being connected with organized crime."

"Wait. I've read about organized crime and the mafia in the casinos, usually in Vegas and in the 1920s, not now."

My dad shook his head. "Not like it was then. Not the same; however, there is organized crime in Vegas, in Atlantic City, and probably other places with extensive legalized gambling. Not all of them. But think about it. Take some rich semi-successful man – or woman – who wants to get richer and doesn't care if people get hurt in the process. They decide to build and open a casino and they need some partners to put up the money. You've been to a casino. They're all about glitz and glamour and appearances. And getting people to come to their casino. Some of their partners may need some place to 'invest' some of their money." He threw up his hands and added "and there you have it."

"Okay, but you're not talking leg breaking or killing people, right?"

He sneered. "Not so you'd know it. Nope, not so you'd know it. And you'd have to be a pretty high roller and lose time after time, and go out on a limb to keep losing, sure you'd recoup it all to warrant any intervention like that. More likely, they'd figure out how to use the sucker to their best interests."

Kevin nodded in agreement. "Not everyone who gambles is an addict. But gambling is an addiction as much as alcoholism or drugs, and people do desperate things to get their fix. My sister's husband was a gambler and when he lost? That's when she ended up in the hospital. When she divorced him, she found out he'd taken out a second mortgage on their home to feed his habit."

My mouth dropped. "I like casino nights and playing penny slots. I go in knowing I'm dropping a hundred bucks or whatever for a good cause. Slots on my computer? For points yes, for money, heck, no."

Our discussion of gambling ended as the laptop sounded its alarm. Kevin turned the screen to my dad. He smiled and stood up. "Nate's here with dinner."

The next few minutes were filled with introductions and lots of groans and sounds that come from even the smell of good Italian food. Nate brought three foil pans – lasagna, sausage and peppers, and chicken cacciatore. And, of course, foil wrapped garlic bread.

"Nate, this is great, but who's gonna eat all this food?"

Nate pointed to my dad. "Wade and Jillian are coming for dinner. And it sounds like you're getting special treatment from the police department here. When they get this all figured out, I suspect you'll have more visitors. They may be hungry."

As if on cue, another notification came on. In unison, Kevin and I both said, "Smythe."

"See. Now you have good food to offer him."

Kevin motioned he'd get the door and my dad asked, "Who's Smythe?"

Nate laughed. "Lionel Smythe is one of my legal cronies."

Kevin and Smythe came into the kitchen with more introductions.

"This all smells so good. Grab a plate, fork and knife, and napkins, and *mange*."

"Ladies first, Stacie, even if you are technically the hostess here." Dad handed me a dish and I didn't hesitate to take a small serving of each, topped off with garlic bread.

While everyone got their dishes, I pulled down wine glasses and Kevin helped open the bottles of wine. My refrigerator might not be full, but my wine cooler was. Wade and Jillian arrived and exclaimed over the food as well. My kitchen isn't intended for a crowd for dinner. We moved the four chairs into the living area to maximize seating capacity and everyone dug in.

CHAPTER 33

Wine and food made for a pleasant evening. Jillian helped me collect all the dishes and get them into the dishwasher.

"Wade said it was a bit tense when your dad got here. Kevin came from the back of the house looking like he'd just woke up."

"They were chatting away by the time I got up. Not sure what Kevin and Wade told him or how they explained anything."

"Wade said they emphasized the idea that you needed to lay low until this was sorted out and they'd agreed one of them needed to stay here with you in case of trouble."

Movement and voices dragged us back to the living area. Detective O'Hare arrived and looked much better.

"Evening. You're having a party and didn't invite me."

"We did save food for you. Have you eaten?"

He hesitated. "No, but I really shouldn't. I offered to come by and update you. Reston PD has been very busy today, as have we."

"You sit down and let me get you a plate. Just a bite won't hurt." My dad nodded and nudged O'Hare toward the big chair he'd vacated.

O'Hare's mouth opened and with a slight head shake he sat down. He scanned all of us and opened his mouth to speak when my dad handed him a plate, utensils, and a napkin.

"I hear you've been very good to my daughter. Enjoy."

O'Hare coughed. "Thank you, Mr. Maroni. This smells wonderful." He looked down and then back up, all of us staring at him. "First things first. We were able to connect the two men from last night with Bryce's office number. When confronted, Bryce indicated her Public Relations person, Randy Checznuf, must be responsible and did her best to separate herself from the situation. She didn't know anything, that was the number he used not her."

"Who is he?"

"What does he have to do with Stacie?"

While we all groaned and reacted, O'Hare managed to eat a couple bites. When we all stopped asking questions, he continued.

"Checznuf confirmed that was the number he was assigned. He answers all calls to her, screens them if you will. When asked about the brothers dumb and the jobs they did for him, he looked confused. He did receive the messages for Bryce of this or that was taken care of, but he assumed it was some errand or something on her house. He recalled one message saying that the garage was all set and then another, it was all done. He had no idea what they were in reference to and simply left her the call note. He produced the telephone message pad with all the messages in carbon and not just from them." He paused for effect.

"Don't keep us in the dark, here. What did you find out?"

"Reston PD shared all the dates and the messages with the calls they responded to and we checked on our end on calls with you. Many were aligned. A few other messages connected to Stewart's calls, one to Meredith Langford's accident report. A couple they're still trying to sort out.

"How'd the good senator explain them?" Wade asked with a sneer.

"She claimed she didn't know anything about them."

"So where does that leave this mess?"

O'Hare ran his hand over his face. "Well, the brothers dumb? When we shared some of those messages with them, they folded. Bryce was the one who called them and directed them what to do. Reston PD has her in custody with a lot more questions."

"Was Ned Anderson one of those 'jobs' she directed?" Killing somebody over a meeting seemed a bit extreme to me.

"There was no message from the brothers dumb on that date and they said they didn't know anything about a man assaulted in the elevator."

"Coincidence?" I asked with disbelief.

O'Hare chuckled. "Not likely, just not resolved as yet."

"I get the feeling there is more," Kevin commented.

"McNair, you are correct and it connects a lot of events. I'll start with the short explanation of Langford's behavior. His wife has some problems, drinking and gambling among them. Langford's done his best to keep this out of the press and try to get his wife the help she needs. Two things complicated the situation. Mrs. Langford has been deemed *persona non grata* at many casinos due to her behavior when she loses and they refuse to front her credit. All except one in Atlantic City with questionable connections to organized crime. They gave her one extension and another, and another, and she keeps playing, and now they want their money."

"I told you I thought I recognized that picture!"

"So how does that connect to the foundation and Bryce?" Clearly, I was missing something.

"I'm guessing that's one of the casinos Bryce is a silent partner in." Smythe offered.

O'Hare nodded. "Not only is she connected to the organized crime part, Bryce threatened to go public with what she knows about Monica Langford's drinking and gambling debts. Langford is weak and aware of how much that would hurt his chances for re-election."

"That explains why he's voting her side but still arguing his position."

"He was in a bad place politically and financially. His wife – and by extension, Langford – is way in debt to the casino. He doesn't have enough money to pay off her debts, and she keeps slipping away from his security. One of the partners in the casino suggested he could pay them off via grant funds. Only he drags his feet. Every time someone has an accident, or there's a problem, he's notified to let him know what could happen to him or his family."

Smythe leaned forward, excited. "All those emails telling him who to convince not to be on the foundation, the award of a grant when there is no grant... All that was orchestrated by organized crime?"

"Bryce again. Chief Rizzo shared that you'd provided emails from someone pulling the strings on this operation. The tech guys at Reston PD were able to trace some of the IP addresses to the nearest cell tower. The most common point was Bryce's office."

"That's not going to hold up in court. She can't be the only one in that building and could argue the calculations are best estimate."

"Good point, Kevin. I'm not sure what else they found. Chief Rizzo shared they had her as complicit if not the person behind the emails based on what was on her computer."

"Good. I'm glad to hear it. Though I do feel bad for Langford. His wife is ill and needs help, only that won't happen until she recognizes she has a problem. When will this be made public?"

"Sticky business when dealing with government officials. There is a lot that has to happen. Technically, it's not clear if Langford has broken the law, other than not reporting what he knew or suspected, and therefore obstructing justice. So far, no charges have been made."

I blurted out, "What about Bryce?"

"Bryce is another story altogether. Until the Reston DA determines the charges against her, it will likely be kept as quiet as possible as she vacates her office and steps are taken with regard to her position, her safety, and ensuring she'll be around to stand trial. I suspect rumors will be flying of her stepping down by tonight or tomorrow. It will probably take another day before more information is shared – her connection to casinos and organized crime front and center. The brothers dumb and harassment of you, Smythe's 'accident,' and other events? Even if mentioned, easily forgotten."

"Now, will you get off that foundation already, Stacie?"

"No, Dad. Someone will have to replace Langford, though, and that won't be me. Once all this funny business is settled, there should be no problems and potentially a lot of good can come from the foundation."

He shook his head and looked to Nate, who shrugged.

O'Hare finished off his food. "Even though you should be safe? Use the alarm and don't hesitate to call. I'm out of here."

I walked him to the door. "Thanks for the special attention, Detective."

He smiled. "My pleasure. See you around."

I walked back in to find my dad, Nate, and Smythe deep in conversation and Wade, Jillian, and Kevin in cahoots. The older trio broke up first.

"Stacie, we're going to take off. Ends up your friend here and Nate and me, we know some of the same people. Gotta catch up on old friends."

"Thanks for coming down and caring. And Nate, thank you so much for bringing dinner. Do you want to take what's left?"

"Stacie, you have plenty of room in your fridge. You and your friends enjoy."

Smythe gave me a one-arm hug. "I'll get in touch with Trichter to figure out the next steps, without Langford."

Dad turned to my friends and gave Jillian a hug. "Wade, good to see you again. Kevin, nice to meet you."

Dad's parting comment to them, pointedly to Kevin was, "I look forward to seeing you at Deanna's and my wedding in January."

EPILOGUE

Life had quieted down over the next week. The announcement of charges against Bryce and her alleged connections to organized crime had lit up the news for a few days, thankfully with no mention of the foundation. Work was steady with the occasional adrenalin rush when there was a crisis.

My Saturday was pretty full. Jasper taken care of, I headed to Cornerstone. Shawna and Layla radiated excitement when I got there.

"What's going on? You both look like it was Christmas and Santa was especially good to you."

"Close, Stacie. The information from Tam and Princess Vi? Her name is Alise, by the way. Yesterday, the detective took them for a ride to see if they could recognize the warehouse or the house where they'd been taken. They did good and narrowed it down to three possible warehouses. The detective was able to get search warrants for all three. In the second one, they found twelve girls, some in pretty bad shape. They're all in the hospital – a couple of them may come here, social work is trying to find a place for the others."

"Did they get the people behind it all?"

Layla spit out. "No. Only one woman was there and she lawyered up. Claimed to not know where the girls came from or where they went."

"What about the man's house? Did they find it?"

Shawna laughed. "That man is really sorry now about his signage proclaiming he had the best kept yard and some famous tree. The girls are in protective custody until the trial. They'll continue to get services and maybe some tutoring. Their families have been notified and the social worker is meeting with them before they are reunited."

"That's the best news ever. It will still be a long road for them and their families. At least they can feel like they had the opportunity to help other girls and testify against the man."

"You have two new women to see. And then I guess we have a lunch meeting with Mr. Smythe and the foundation board." She rolled her eyes and I laughed.

I met with the women who'd been there for a while and touched base with the two new women. As I left, I joked with Shawna, "Hey, maybe you'll be the next Chair of the board."

"Not in this lifetime. And you better not either. Hold up a second, I'm gonna follow you."

I pulled into the hotel parking lot and waited on Shawna. We found our way to the conference room, catered for lunch. I was surprised to see Mr. Trichter, as well as Mr. Smythe. Other than Jacob, no one else had arrived yet.

"Hi Stacie, Shawna. Please help yourself and have a seat."

By the time we had our food and sat down, others trickled in. Chief Rizzo made a point to stop. "I trust the bad karma has settled down?"

"Most definitely. Thanks for all you did. What I still don't understand is what happened to Ned?"

He exhaled and spoke quietly. "The two guys at your house? They weren't the only ones on the payroll. Some basic police work and phone messages – we got the man who killed him. It was no mugging and no coincidence."

I nodded and wondered at the effects the trial would have on Kayla and her baby. The chief walked away and Kevin walked in, smiled, and brushed his hand over my shoulder on his way to get his food. Austin Beasley and J. Colton Stewart came in after that along with Dr. Hanreddy, Alexa Morales, and Tyler Kearns. No Chief Petkra. Interesting.

Mr. Smythe tapped a class with his spoon. "Good afternoon. Please help yourself to lunch and hot and cold beverages. As you may or may not be aware, Senator Langford has stepped down from the foundation. Both Senator Bryce and Chief Petkra will no longer be on the board due to significant conflicts of interest."

He paused before he continued. "Allow me to introduce Mr. Cyrus Trichter, Theodore Noth's attorney."

"Good afternoon. In the codicil, Ted specifically named Senator Langford to serve as chairman of the board due to their work together, unless of course he declined or was unable to serve. He didn't identify a second choice. Mr. Smythe and I have considered this situation and two things come to mind. First, the chairperson needs to be able to deal with the public effectively, have a vested interest in the good the foundation was intended to foster, and have strong public relations skills. Second, the chairperson should be elected by the remaining members of the board, and then the three remaining seats filled."

We all looked around the room and waited.

"What is the next step?"

"Is there a nomination of anyone in the room?"

Kevin cleared his throat. "I nominate Austin Beasley. He represents the NFL, a prominent voice recently in addressing domestic violence, and he has those people skills you referred to like nobody else I know."

"Is there a second?"

"Second." I smiled at Shawna's quick response.

"Mr. Beasley, are you willing to take on the leadership of this committee? We will understand if you need to check with the NFL. You might point out though that as chair, you would only have a vote in the case of a tie."

"I would be honored to take on the leadership. I will need to check though to be sure the Sports Commission doesn't have an issue."

"Fair enough. Any other nominations?"

"Hearing none, we will table a vote on Chairperson until we hear from Mr. Beasley. We would like to discuss the open seats on the board and any suggestions. One female, and two males. Mr. Dimbody has been found to have a conflict so he will not be reconsidered. As should have occurred, vetting of the potential members of the board will be completed by Mr. Stewart and Ms. Maroni, but this time only after completion of thorough background checks."

There was some discussion and suggestions of possible members offered. Two hours later and the meeting was adjourned. I joked with Shawna as we left and she kept looking for Beasley.

"Hey, he seems like a nice guy. My friend Jillian described him as 'cuddly' – he does resemble a big teddy bear."

She laughed. "And Mr. Blue Eyes?"

I smiled. "We have our official first date tonight. Dinner at La Bella Vita. And I need to get home and get dressed."

AUTHOR NOTES

Thank you for reading *Foundations, Funny Business & Murder*. I hope you enjoyed it.

About Christa Nardi

Christa Nardi is an avid reader with her love of mysteries beginning with Nancy Drew and the Dana Girls. She loves a good mystery, especially if there are dogs. Her favorite authors have shifted to more contemporary mystery and crime authors over time, cozy and traditional. Christa has been a long time writer from poetry and short stories to mystery series. Christa is a member of Sisters in Crime.

You can find Christa Nardi on most social media. You can contact her at cccnardi@gmail.com.
Check out her blog - Christa Reads and Writes (https://www.christanardi.blogspot) or sign up for her monthly newsletter (http://smarturl.it/NardiNewsletter)

Be sure you don't miss any of the Stacie Maroni Mysteries by Christa Nardi:
Prestige, Privilege & Murder *(A Stacie Maroni Mystery #1)* – Divorce papers served, Stacie finds herself a suspect in her estranged husband's murder.
Foundations, Funny Business & Murder *(A Stacie Maroni Mystery #2)* – Stacie discovers that even good intentions and a foundation can be marred by funny business.
Deception, Denial & Murder *(A Stacie Maroni Mystery #3)* – Tension in the work place and romantic relationships lead Stacie to be involved in another murder.
Holidays, Hijinks & Murder *(A Stacie Maroni Holiday Mystery)* – Coming in 2010.

Other Series by Christa Nardi

Sheridan Hendley Mysteries
The Cold Creek Series
The Hannah and Tamar Mysteries for Young Adults with Cassidy Salem

Printed in Great Britain
by Amazon